OPPOS

Gwendoline Riley was born in 1979 and has published three previous novels: *Cold Water*, which won a Betty Trask Award; *Sick Notes*; and *Joshua Spassky*, which was shortlisted for the John Llewellyn Rhys Prize and won the Somerset Maugham Award.

ALSO BY GWENDOLINE RILEY

Cold Water
Sick Notes
Joshua Spassky

GWENDOLINE RILEY

Opposed Positions

VINTAGE BOOKS
London

Published by Vintage 2014

2 4 6 8 10 9 7 5 3 1

First published in Great Britain in 2012 by
Jonathan Cape

Vintage
Random House, 20 Vauxhall Bridge Road,
London SW1V 2SA

www.vintage-books.co.uk

Addresses for companies within The Random House Group Limited
can be found at: www.randomhouse.co.uk/offices.htm

The Random House Group Limited Reg. No. 954009

A CIP catalogue record for this book
is available from the British Library

ISBN 9780099565192

The Random House Group Limited supports the Forest Stewardship
Council® (FSC®), the leading international forest-certification organisation.
Our books carrying the FSC label are printed on FSC®-certified paper.
FSC is the only forest-certification scheme supported by the leading
environmental organisations, including Greenpeace. Our
paper procurement policy can be found at:
www.randomhouse.co.uk/environment

Typeset in Bembo by Palimpsest Book Production Limited
Falkirk, Stirlingshire

Printed and bound in Great Britain by Clays Ltd, St Ives plc

Did fiction do this to me?

Philip Roth

I

1

I think this happened on their first date: when she came back from the Ladies' to find him talking about her. He was boasting to his two brothers, telling now how he'd had to use his pull to get her her job.

'Yes, I might well live to regret it!' he was saying.

And: 'No, it wasn't an easy sell, that!'

And it would have been – quite a feat, he was right. Him having worked in their office for what, six weeks? While she'd been there for two years, since she'd graduated. But no matter, passing her over her drink, he went on, to say that she was pretty hopeless all round, really. With the practical side of things, did they see? The way a business *works* . . .

His brothers were visiting for the weekend. Their first time down in London, from Sheffield, they would have been – still quite shy, I imagine, and quiet until they were drunk. Not up to much eye contact with her, anyway, I wouldn't have thought, as with his arm around her again now, he jiggled her, saying, 'This one couldn't wire a *plug* before she met me!'

She married him because: 'Well, it was just what you did.'

'He had all those brothers. It seemed like a ready-made, nice, big family. My childhood was *so lonely* with just me.'

'Oh, I don't know. Women got married and had babies. It wasn't like today, so — aren't you lucky, hey?'

She called my questions funny. They were funny. She would keep answering them, though, so I learned all about it. How he 'banned' her from wearing trousers, for instance. She said that very matter-of-factly, too.

'Hold on,' I said. '*Banned?*'

'Oh, yes.' She nodded.

It went further than that, though. The weekend after their honeymoon, while she was out at the supermarket, he took it upon himself to gather her trousers up. Again, I picture him: standing there with his arms full. I think he must have got anxious, mustn't he? Left alone in that new flat, going from room to room. (I even think I

4

can hear his breathing as he did that.) I imagine him thinking something like, having this – wife now, what else could he have? When she got back he showed her what he'd done before she'd even put the shopping down. That's almost touching, isn't it? Wanting her to see, her clothes there in a bin bag – and covered in paint, too: he'd poured a good long goop of white paint in there with them; the last of what they'd used in the hall.

He liked to take photographs, too. I know that was a craze for a while. Whenever she was harried or un-made-up would do: when she was cooking, or when she was ill. When she was on the toilet was a favourite. (He unscrewed the lock from the bathroom door the day they moved in.)

When the films came back he'd sit at the dining table and go through each set, passing her the ones he thought were funniest. (The ones where she looked the worst.)

'Oof!' he'd say.

And when she didn't laugh: 'Sulking!'

And all night long: 'Oh! She's still sulking!'

So she was in those photographs, and she was sitting at the table with him, and then – she was somewhere else entirely, too, I had to assume. That would be the way to deal with a situation like that, wouldn't it? I mean, I've been prone to that myself, I know: drifting off.

'Well, I was still heartbroken over Anthony, I think, looking back,' she said, 'wasn't I? When he left I wanted to die. I barely knew what I was doing.'

And: 'Well, he didn't hit me until after we were married, did he? And then I had no job any more, and then I had you two kiddies. He controlled everything, all the money. He used to say I was welcome to go but, oh, I could never take you. He'd *kill* us all first.'

'Right,' I said. 'Okay.'

I remember the day we left: that surprise reprieve from school when I'd already put on my uniform: a grey shirt tucked into grey wool tights, and then that bottle-green tunic. I was tugged out of them, and then tugged into my weekend clothes, my coat and my wellingtons, and told to sit still in the living room. From the window in there I watched Mum struggle out with bag after bag, down the path, back and forth between our building and an estate car that I didn't recognise. That done, she strapped my brother Liam into his buggy.

'Well, come on then,' she said.

Our progress was slow. The roads were icy, and then the motorway jammed. I remember Mum peering into the rear-view, her chin up, her teeth bared. At lunchtime we stopped at a Little Chef. Not that I wanted to eat, particularly, and Mum's attempt at her beans on toast amounted to only a couple of over-chewed mouthfuls before she put her cutlery down and wiped her mouth.

'Now don't complain if you get hungry later,' she said.

It got dark quickly after that, and I got tired, and soon I was being woken up again, this time outside Grandma and Grandpa's house, which was in Tyldesley, near Wigan. I'd been there twice before. Getting out of the car, I saw decorations already up in some of the other houses on their street: fairy lights in bay windows blurred by frost and net curtains.

Grandma held the door open and ushered us into the hall, and then into the warm back parlour; Mum carrying Liam and dragging his buggy up the step, and then she went back, and there was that spotty procession of suitcases and bin bags that she left in the hallway and then Grandpa carried upstairs.

Another memory – this must have been a few weeks later, it was a Saturday night, and – Grandma spotted this first: Dad had parked up outside the house.

'Oh, *good God*,' she said.

And then, having gone back to look again through the curtains in the dark front room, 'Still there!' she called out. 'Still there! Oh, that bugger. What's he playing at?'

She kept going to look and then reporting back like that.

Grandpa even decided he was going to go and have a word; he put his coat on, but then he couldn't find his gloves.

'Help me out, Peggy,' he said.

They both fussed furiously, under siege, while Mum sat with us in the back, her feet (in her new Christmas slipper-socks) up on the sofa, watching the TV. There was a three-bar electric fire in there (giving out a fearsome, dry, headachey heat), and a stack of *Reader's Digest*s, and a huge beanbag I considered my own, and a rough tartan blanket that I liked to pull right up over myself, over my head.

'Oh *don't*,' Mum called out eventually. 'Don't give him the satisfaction. Why are you all so excited?'

2

Strapped in, in the back of that car, every Saturday we were taken on the rounds, to various relatives' houses and flats, around Sheffield and Chesterfield. Dad would draw up at nine o'clock, having travelled up the night before and stayed with one of his brothers. He was always on time, and if we were late coming out he'd start sounding his horn: short blasts at first, then longer ones.

'Oh, *Christ*,' Grandma would say. 'Christ *almighty*.'

I remember walking down the path with Liam and seeing him sitting there. He was always only staring straight ahead.

A favourite topic of conversation during that first year, while sitting in one or other of his brothers' front rooms, were the plans he'd had to snatch us. One had been to drive up the motorway in the Routemaster bus his brother Joe worked on, and then wait outside our school in it.

'Imagine that,' he said. 'All your mates seeing you leave in a big red bus! We were going to take you abroad, where your mother couldn't find you!'

He watched for our reaction then; there wasn't much of one, though, and so he shook his head disgustedly, and harrumphed.

'You know,' he said, 'Joe said you were stuck up.'

And: 'You're a prig,' he said, nodding over at me. And then, 'Isn't she?' he said, his attention on Liam now. 'Miss Prig!'

It went on like that. Every Friday night dread infected me. He always looked so starving, and so greedy. That was difficult to bear, I found. And in general his behaving as if certain things were the case with me which were not the case.

Mum said, 'Oh well, you know he's mad; ignore him.

'Saturday's my day,' she said. 'It's my *one day* to get anything done around here.'

He liked to talk about her, though, often as soon as we got into the car, and then he would lean back between the seats when we were stopped at the traffic lights, making sure we got his point, or if not that we knew he was watching us in the rear-view mirror, we saw his eyes letter-boxed there.

'So, er, my spies have seen your mother out and about with my look-alike!' he said one morning.

His 'spies' were the two of his brothers who lived and worked in Liverpool, where Mum now had a job, and where we were hoping to move to soon. Round at his brother Gerry's house later, he told the story again.

'Yes, Calum keeps seeing her out and about with my look-alike, apparently. Hear me, Ged? Calum, yes; he said it was extraordinary. He looks just like me this latest one!'

I think I was ten years old then, sitting there at another kitchen table, drinking another glass of Coke. Dad was sitting opposite me, Liam to his left. They both had pint glasses of Coke, too.

'Of course, your mother's very messed up, you know, in that department,' Dad said. 'I *think* she's probably quite masochistic . . . She had a strange relationship with your grandfather. It had these *undertones*. That's why she likes Clark Gable so much. There's a definite resemblance there. Clark Gable and, er, what's the other one? *Vincent Price*.'

For clarity's sake – honestly, Grandpa looked nothing like Clark Gable. Short, and short-sighted, too, and always so nervous and friendly, I'd liken him to Kenneth Connor, at best.

But then: 'He killed thousands of innocent people, you know, during the war. Children. *Dehousing.* Heh! Yes, you should ask him about that. Ask him about the bombing. The dead children. I'll be *interested* to hear what he has to say!'

Later, when I started to do well at senior school, Dad got into the habit of taking me aside for more confidential conversations. Catching me in hallways, or when Liam was in the bathroom, he'd say, 'You should be careful around your brother, you know.'

Or, 'Boys are funny, you know. And he's not clever in the way *you're* clever.'

('Boys are funny.' Yes, Mum used to say that, too, didn't she?)

'Those who can't, teach!' Dad said. 'You should say that, next time! They're nothing in the outside world, these people. They're losers, to use your brother's word. Those who can, do. You can tell them I said that. Heh!'

I didn't appreciate any of this, but never mind, because soon enough he was leaning back in another one of his brothers' armchairs and saying, 'Of course, there is an argument that the *really* clever people don't go to university. Some of these people with degrees are real thickos. You'll find that. It's the art of the bluff.'

This was round at his brother Niall's house, one afternoon.

'What do you mean?' I said. I could ask him things like that when we were in company.

He raised his eyebrows at Liam and Niall.

'Ooh, whoops, *sorry*. Somebody's sensitive, here! Are you saying you never bluff? Oh, you used to!'

I shook my head.

'No I didn't.'

'Whatever you say!'

And again he reached over, gripped my shoulder and jiggled me.

'Just because I don't pick you up on things, don't think you've ever got one over on *me*. Of course I'm very proud of my *literary* daughter, going off to do her *literary* degree, as you keep reminding us all. I'm interested in what you'll have to do to get it! Ho ho!'

Driving us back home, we passed through Sheffield city centre. The steep pavements were always crowded. It was the women Dad saw.

'Hunting in packs!' he'd say, as we slowed in traffic, or waited at a zebra crossing.

'Oof!' he'd say, craning his neck. 'See that, Liam?'

And if any of the women looked overweight, it was: 'Jesus wept!'

Or: 'Well-fed specimen there!'

He went on, as we pulled away, again talking to us in the rear-view mirror.

'Although some men like that kind of thing. *Some men* . . . They do go for that. You hear that, back there? If you ever feel like putting on a few pounds!'

And what was it my dad 'went for'? I began to wonder. There'd been no indication that he'd had any girlfriends since Mum (or before, now I think of it). I went through a phase as a teenager where I thought he'd frightened himself with the way he'd behaved towards her and made a decision to retreat. Hadn't he had a violent father himself, who he'd hated? That came to seem a rather revolting theory, though. A rather ingratiating idea, really, for me to have been so wistfully espousing to myself. (It makes me angry to think about that now, that I could have had such a lapse of taste. And am I still having them I wonder.)

I asked Mum once, 'Did he ever manage to make any friends, or has it always just been his brothers?'

'Did he?' she said. 'Oh, I don't know. At work, I

suppose. Or did he? I can't remember. I know I felt sorry for him when we first met because he was telling me about a Chinese restaurant he liked because it did a very good set menu for *one*. I thought, *Ah . . .*'

'Right,' I said. 'Very touching. And then, next thing you know: don't wear trousers, and he's thumping you if you look at him wrong.'

'Mm . . .' Mum said.

And then she said, 'Well, it's a long time ago now, isn't it? Not the most pleasant subject matter, this, is it, Aislinn?'

'No,' I said.

When I was seventeen and Liam fifteen, the two of us did at least agree to start dividing the labour. Every other week I stayed at home to revise. ('Oh, you need to revise, do you? I thought you knew it all!' Dad said.) And once a fortnight Liam pleaded football practice and I went alone. (With Dad pointing out, 'Of course, if he had any *real* talent it would have been picked up on long ago. They spot it very early if it's there.')

The last time was a special excursion. Late because of the weather, we sped up on the wet M60, barrelling down the fast lane. The rain bristled thickly on the tarmac and dragged across the windscreen, beading into tiny, dirty pearls. I couldn't get the radio to work. I had kept trying. At last I said, 'I've not been to one of these before.'

Dad harrumphed.

'I know you haven't,' he said. 'That's why I'm taking you.'

'I had to borrow Mum's coat.'

He turned his head sharply then and looked at the coat.

'Oh,' he said, 'well – that's a myth, you know, about wearing black. There are a lot of myths about funerals. You just have to look smart, wear *dark* clothing.'

I nodded.

'Oh, well,' I said.

But he continued to look put out, frowning, and with his mouth turned down at the corners, until at last he said, 'Yes, that's quite an old-fashioned idea actually, about wearing black. I'm *surprised* your mother would say that. *Hm* . . .'

I had the big Collins road atlas open on my knees, ready for every junction, where he'd call out, 'Navigator!'

At the City Road Cemetery the last tears leaked slowly out of Aunt Fran's bloodshot eyes. Aunt

Fran, in her black boots, a black coat and a black crushed-velvet hat. She looked like she'd been spat at. And her daughter, too, my cousin, little Michaela, her round, yoghurt-and-jam complex-ioned face was a strange, small study in impassive fatigue, as she watched the coffin being let down. The box held Fran's second husband, of only six months, a man I hadn't ever met. In fact, there weren't any other Kellys among the mourners: only Dad and me. I recognised Fran's sister and her husband, and then there were two burlier, older men, one of whom had given a eulogy as a representative of the Sheffield Trades Union Council. Those men were well into their sixties, I guessed, with those tusking eyebrows and pendant earlobes – but still, they looked tough. They kept their baggy jaws set. I'd seen Dad around men like them before. Something about their type – their authority, maybe, their stout gruffness – made him stand up straighter; excited him, or shamed him, somehow, it seemed. Like a small boy might get excited, or feel ashamed, and stand up straighter for it. Trying to be noticed? Or trying not to be noticed? I wasn't sure. It was curious, though.

After the committal everybody bowed their heads and I took off my coat and held it over my arm. The rain had stopped and I felt too hot. (It was hot, the grave even seemed to be steaming now; the vapour rising bright and silvery against the sodden earth.) Dad looked me over again then, as I looked down, and then he leaned in and whispered, '*You look a million dollars.*'

At the wake he leaned in closer still, nodding towards the young priest who was standing by the buffet table now, placidly munching on a mini pizza. (Behind him, through the patio doors, I could see the sky clearing over the valley, the clouds burning away . . .)

'He doesn't look the smartest, does he?' Dad said. 'But then they're all pretty nasty pieces of work, though, that lot.'

'Mm . . .' I said.

He went and poured himself a glass of sherry from the sideboard next. Walking back across the parlour he stuck his tongue out at me. His face was flushed and eager. His dripping, royal blue anorak was still zipped right up. Had we even been invited here? I began to wonder. Nobody had seemed very keen to talk to us when we'd arrived at the church, or here, the last in that slow convoy up the hill to the Hutcliffe Estate.

Dad mused on that, on the long drive back.

'You lost some points this afternoon, you

know,' he said. 'A *few* people mentioned it to me. It's just a certain expression on your face. Maybe you can't help it, I don't know. But you need to work on it. Understand? It doesn't go down well with people, all this *posing*. Are you taking this in? You don't look like you are.'

When we stopped at a junction he started prodding the top of my arm.

'You're doing it now!' he said. 'Posing!'

But that came later. For now he sat back down next to me in the corner, adjusting his trousers as he surveyed the bustle. We both sat there looking out at the room; the neighbours who were arriving and asking after Fran. Dad watched them, and huffed. And then, when he tasted his drink, he pulled a face. The same face from before, in the car. This did seem to be happening a lot, didn't it? The cicerone, slighted. I watched him draw himself up there, as we continued to be ignored, until he looked very haughty, like some slandered schoolmistress in an old film.

'Yes, it's a *funny* thing, religion . . .' he said at last.

The next Saturday it was my turn to stay at home. I stayed in my bedroom all afternoon, lying on my bed and reading. I was reading, and writing a little. (I started by writing notes inside the back covers of my books.) It was nine o'clock before the phone rang. I went down and answered it in the hall.

'I tried to show him,' Dad said, and then he sobbed, 'He wasn't even looking around!'

Again: *sob sob*.

'Hello?' I said.

'I had to give him a little punch and he ran off! Is he there?'

'No,' I said.

Liam's face was a mess when he did appear (I heard his key catch the lock just before ten, he'd taken a train back) with his left eye swollen closed and dark blood crusted around his nostrils. His open eye looked relaxed, though. I quite fancied the look in that eye, before I stood aside, for him to walk ahead of me down the hallway, yawning first, and then saying, yeah, he was pretty sure one of his ribs was cracked, too.

Hearing us talking, Mum came down from her bedroom. She was rubbing her eyes. She did look tired.

'Oh, what have you said to him now?' she said. 'Oh, now you *know* you mustn't provoke him . . .'

Liam finally told me properly a few days later how he'd spent that afternoon, being driven slowly around the back streets of Attercliffe, where Dad had grown up.

'*This* is how people live,' he'd said, as they'd rolled past two-up, two-down terraces, and betting shops, and chip shops, and dark, vinegary pubs . . . Dad had even pointed out the local toughs, driving with one hand on the steering wheel, the other draped over the back of Liam's seat.

Liam did a good impression of that; tipping his head back and drawing his newly thick, newly dark, thatched eyebrows together. The effect was even more provocative now, with all those vari-coloured bruises, I mean. So −

'Look at them,' he'd said. 'Look. You're not looking!'

Were these the boys he wished Liam was like? I wondered. Boys like he had been, maybe. Him and his brothers, out and about. Or boys like he'd never been? That seemed more likely, didn't it? But − who knew? Who cared, in fact? No, Liam's impulse, too, was to shrug. An impulse he didn't bother to suppress this time. And why should he, after all?

So that had been that. The car began drifting towards the kerb . . .

Our dad's face could bloom so quickly into

fury, I remember: bloom and collapse at the same time, so that they seemed like the same thing, that triumph and that terror, his eyes wide and his face flooded with hot colour, once he'd taken in any perceived slight, or sedition, from his children . . .

So even as he was jerking the handbrake on, there would have been that. And then those grabbing fists, struggling with Liam over the seatbelt first, then over the door handle, which when it finally gave left Liam half in and half out, and with both of his hands skinned. From there he'd crawled forward and kicked out. I even pictured him laughing then; the cool air in his lungs suddenly, his eyes watering.

3

Meanwhile, for me, there was university in September: I studied English at UCL, living for the first six months in a tiny, wipe-down room in halls, before moving into a flat in Tufnell Park, with a rotating cast of Greek and Spanish girls who were always out, which was fine by me. I used to wait by my bedroom door, checking the kitchen was quiet before I went down and made my vegetables every night. I rarely went out myself; I knew nobody. I spoke up in my seminars, but otherwise I could say that I fell very pleasantly and peaceably mute for those three years.

Hauling carrier bags of books home from the charity shop by the station, I read at night. These books piled up around the walls, and the ones I didn't appreciate I took downstairs and dropped in the outside bin; let them bloat in the bilge there, their toast-brown pages turning to fins. My curiosity did not extend at all beyond what I could discern through these books. It didn't need to. When I was reading, responding to a novel or a poem, there was something there that I trusted, I found. (And liked, as it goes.) Writing was trickier, but again, sometimes there was something there. Every now and then. And I couldn't call that my 'sensibility', at last I had to call it my self, that equivocal calibration; that something-and-nothing.

Having looked back over those old books since, what I've found are: underlinings that I don't understand, asterisked passages that don't seem exceptional (despite the vehemence in their marking up!). Inside their back covers, again, there are the first bits of writing I was doing: some sentences, half-sentences, pairs of words. These, too, don't make much sense to me any more. They seem – unmoored, also – strident somehow. It's hard to tell what I was getting at, only that – clearly there was *something* I was trying to sound out, and that was how I had to start, apparently, with that kind of calling out.

I moved up to Manchester to do my MA. I had a friend there, Cathy, who'd been on my English course (for two terms anyway, before she dropped out). She lived in Withington and cleared out her spare room for me.

With only my slow old word processor between us up there, and with the noise from the bar downstairs a nuisance, I often used to work in the university library. I set up my first email account there, too, at the beginning of term. Not that I got much mail at first: there were some mailshots, I had a note from my mum, and one from Cathy (sent from the computer next to mine on the day we both signed up). Both had had the subject line: *Testing!* After a few weeks there was one other friend with whom I settled into a regular correspondence. I'd try to write to him every Friday afternoon, when the Media Centre was quiet. I'd write to him, and then do some of my own work. I was often the last person to leave.

The other messages – the ones from my dad – started a few months later, just after the Christmas break. (My name was in a directory on the MMU site, I realised later.) This was the first one I opened:

Brian Kelly *Naughty girl!*
You may consider yourself too old to be called such, but it is very easy to see you as childish.

'How strange,' Mum said. (I'd phoned her up immediately.) 'Now calm down, Ash. Tell me again.'

'Oh, now, I wonder what's triggered this. Are you sure you haven't had any other contact?'

'No,' I said. 'I've just told you I haven't.'

I was speaking far too loudly, pacing around the landing of the library stairwell now, with my voice echoing back to me.

'Oh, calm down,' Mum said, 'calm down. Don't shout at *me*. I'm in *work*. Do you want to ring me this evening?'

I tried to calm down, but I didn't manage it, I'm afraid. Had he been trying to get in touch? Was that why he was taking this tone? Were there unopened letters at an old address? The idea almost instantly revealed itself as absurd. What would my dad write in a letter? Where would he summon that kind of self-control? And what would it explain anyway? It wouldn't explain this 'Naughty girl' business, which I had no intention of replying to. He wrote again anyway, of course. I knew he would. I went in to the library first thing Monday morning and checked, and got this for my trouble:

Brian Kelly *Naughty **little** girl!*
Is that better?
Come on now, stop teasing me! Where are you?

And then this arrived. It arrived while I was sitting there, which was unnerving:

Brian Kelly *In Purdah!*
Okay. What am I supposed to have done now? I was brought up Catholic you know, I always feel guilty!

They just kept coming after that, often several a week, and sent at all hours of the day (I was very stupid, I started checking every day. I fell for that). So I got:

Brian Kelly *Teasing*
*Ah, I see, do you **want** me to come looking? You only have to ask! Don't be coy!*

Brian Kelly *Pout*
I can just picture you. Stop sulking.

Brian Kelly *fool*
Do you think I'm interested? Dream on!

Brian Kelly *My files*
Bury your head in the sand but it is clear you are doing something you don't want me to know and certainly don't want to talk to me about. You're kidding yourself. Childish.

Cathy said, 'Christ, Aislinn! You should block him!'

Mum said, 'Oh, it sounds like he's gone mad. Can't you just ignore him?'

Both reasonable suggestions. More than reasonable. But – well, for one thing, I couldn't find a way to block people in that account. That's a practical point of the kind that's often easily dismissible, isn't it? It didn't feel dismissible, though. There really wasn't a way to block individual addresses. And I didn't want to close my account. Why should I have to do that? As to ignoring him, my mum's helpful tip: that was difficult to do as well. I think I was fixed, in a way, or – I don't know what to call it, as the messages kept coming, and their tone started to really spasm. I mean, it turns out to be quite the spectacle, doesn't it? A man not responded to.

Brian Kelly *Sensible shoes!*
Do you where sensible shoes? I don't care if your a lesbian. Your mother and I knew from Day One. Do what you want.

('What's he bringing me into this for?' Mum said.)

Brian Kelly *I despair!*
You'll wind up alienating all kinds of people with behaviour like this. Cheap theatrics. Fool.

Brian Kelly *that Greer woman*
As you may recall I have been telling anyone who'll listen that Germaine's credibility was vanishing, that she was past her sell by date. Just been listening to Woman's hour and I begin to feel she's been a con all her life. She has just said she is sixty (2 years older than me!) and I don't believe that.

Certainly I was frightened, and not because I thought he was going to 'come looking', as he kept saying. The incontinence was frightening to me. And the rapacity. And the gloating and toddler-ish glee taken in both. Also, there was that very familiar feeling from childhood, of being both his sole focus (for attack or attention), and also completely disregarded: my personality, I mean, my boundaries, my independent existence, all valued at nil. My opening of that email account seemed to have functioned as a 'tuning in' to that treatment, and to those assumptions. And why? Because I'd used my real name, and in doing so, in however oblique a way, I'd made myself available. Because of who I was, this

29

was what I got. That was hard to think my way out of.

Brian Kelly *tasty soup recipe*
Are you still pretending to be a vegetarian?
Thought not!
Ask your butcher for these . . .

Brian Kelly *'A fathers thoughts'*
Oh come on. What now? You can tell me. Has another one dumped you?

Brian Kelly *Aw Diddums!*
Ooh! Did I kick a corn?

Brian Kelly *What did YOU do wrong?*
The admissions process for Oxbridge continues to fascinate. Interesting read here . . .

The subject lines of several messages I received in one morning read:

Thoughts of you
Thinking of you
Still thinking
Thinking
Rarely out of my mind

Ah
As so often: thoughts of you.

Each message was one of Shakespeare's sonnets. *Studies continue!* he wrote.

At times like that, I did wonder about replying, sending something neutral, like, *Hi Dad, No, I'm not sulking, just really busy working at the moment. Hope you're well.* (To be kind, you understand, and to keep him at bay; a quaint notion that seems now.) But then I'd log in to something that made me less inclined to do that, really. To the other kinds of message, the ones that would stoke a growing dis-ease with whatever the hell it was that I was made up of. The freckles on my arms, I remember, so like the freckles that smutted his forearms, began to be a particular torment to me at this time. The colour of my hair, too, became a problem again, and the way my face looked in repose. I started to carry myself quite differently, trying to ward all of that off.

Brian Kelly *OOH!*
Showing off again are we?

Brian Kelly *Your problem?*
Women (who can do 2 things at once) are notorious

for their lack of imagination. Harry Potter is a famous exception.

Brian Kelly *Navigator*
I went on a driving holiday back to Scotland this weekend (up to Ullapool, remember?). Could have done with my trusty navigator! The 'fried Mars bar' tendency is in full effect up there (even in the ★★★★(★) establishments.) Sugar in the gravy! Cheese boards served with a sugary chutney! I refused all puddings. It seems I am losing my taste for sweets, and not a moment too soon!

Brian Kelly *Am I alone?*
Beyond despair!

Brian Kelly *Inheritance*
Goes down the male line. There's nothing in it for **you** *if I die!*

Month after month, all these sullen retreats and these roaring returns. Yet I could never be sure how much of what he wrote had anything to do with him: how real these assertions were, how merely habitual, or − innate; or was this all just a nasty, idle hobby for him now, in fact? (Because that can happen, can't it? I mean, it's happened to me, I know, I've slipped my tracks with people, with work sometimes, too.) But there was no way of knowing. My instinct was the same as it had been when I was small: that he was more contraption than person. So what could I do? It didn't feel like it was my business to do anything, when I received a message like this, for instance:

Brian Kelly *Feeling distressed*
I am sick of being abused by you and your mother.

A message without meaning, without any relation to the real world. This one particularly seemed to speak of a self-abasement that I couldn't begin to understand. I really couldn't. I could try . . . But why was that my job? I told Cathy and Mum. I'd taken to phoning both of them and reading these messages out, as soon as I received them. Mum said, 'Oh dear. How *strange*.' Cathy said, 'Block him! Erase him from your life!'

Brian Kelly *In Denial*
I don't know who you think you are. I remember when you liked Michael Jackson.

Brian Kelly *My lawyer*
Has now sent me my files. So much I'd forgotten,

obliterated. Your mothers accusations even more obscene! When I have access to fax I send.

He was distracted from that line of thought, though, when I had a book out that spring. I heard nothing from him for a few weeks after that. And when I did (with my new computer – in our living room now – even giving a pert, doorbell-y *ping* to herald his bright, renewed suit):

Brian Kelly *The font!*
I like the font. Nothing else!

This being very plausibly and reasonably the case, he nonetheless typed up several quotes and sent them to me, annotated:

Oh dear!
Oof!
Posing!
Er, what?

And then:

Brian Kelly *Smelly daughter.*
*Pouting are we? I can just picture you. Ah. Why so sensitive? Am I not **allowed** an opinion? I was*

reading before you were born remember. If we assume
*we both started **seriously** reading at 10, I have forty*
plus years on you!

Brian Kelly *However . . .*
I want my signed, dedicated copy of this 'novel' by
first post.

Brian Kelly *Thcweam and thcweam!*
Do you think I'm interested in your miniature
drama? Dream on. Send the book.

Brian Kelly *Cruel*
I think you're being very cruel.

Brian Kelly *My Death*
Only ocurred in your book. In reality, I live on!

Did he, though? This fraught ravening at my
dusty computer screen . . . Was that life? As it
went on, I began rather to think of him as the
dying – although I wasn't sure what that
made me. I think maybe it made me – nothing.
There was a role he wanted to manoeuvre me
into, certainly. But that wasn't me. The trouble
was, as ever, that – because he'd take anything,
grab at anything and co-opt it – my inaction

was taken as assent. And what a quicksand that was. I did nothing and was railed against. I did nothing and became more tormenting, and therefore – grotesquely – more *supreme*. I felt that happening. I then felt this imagined supremacy itself becoming a kind of gasped-after salve: each lack of reply now taken as another messy recrudescence tenderly cauterised; a fretful appeal gracefully denied; another craven strategy tactfully dismantled. That was how he set me up. So he wrote that he was *very poorly*.

Feeling shattered! he said. And I didn't reply. So then he wrote that he'd had a job offer in South America. *It deserves serious consideration*, he wrote. And I didn't reply. So it was back to the hospital, and the nurses:

> *With some of these women, I often wonder if they have much better paid jobs on the phone at home. It is (still) quite shocking to discover / realise / have it confirmed yet again, how easy it is for women to sound sexy, entising, seductive. Deceit, thy name is woman!*

Then it was back to the job:

I hesitate, and their terms become more attractive.
But money isn't the only consideration. There are
several considerations.

There wasn't much to hold on to. Perhaps only
an idea that the dying – because they can't help
what they become either – might, in fact, hate what
they found themselves to be. Perhaps they were
even ashamed of it. Perhaps he and I shared that.
But no –

Brian Kelly *Access*
I fought your mother and the courts to gain access
to you. **You** *will be easy compared to them!*

'God, are you okay?' Cathy said, coming back in
from the kitchen with our two drinks. 'Your face
has gone all red.'

4

Perhaps it's a Hollywood myth, how this happens, but I know I've seen more than a few war movies featuring the following tense sequence: a soldier making his way through enemy territory hears a faint click at his feet and freezes, knowing he's stepped on a mine, and knowing, too, that the thing will detonate, it will *tear him open*, the second he steps off it. That's become the decision he has to make. Unless – can he try to weight the thing with his pack? Would that be heavy enough? Or how about a real ersatz Zeus: is there a rock nearby he can reach for?

This felt a useful metaphor to me back then, anyway, life seeming once again to be pretty well rigged; my ongoing existence being assessed again, apparently, as an impiety, a de facto infraction. And similarly, too – it occurred to me – escape would require a substitutionary sleight, a well-weighted illusion left in my stead. Then everyone could be happy. (There's something like that in the Bible, too, isn't there? 'Love does not discriminate.')

I'm not talking about 'shedding a skin' here. Rather removing yourself – one way or another, however you can – from a system where you have no viability.

It was with this in mind – at least, I think I had it in mind, a mission to jam the apparatus, somehow – that the Saturday after I got that email, the last weekend in August, I took the train down to London, and then the tube out to Fulham, to visit my dad. (Of course, another way of looking at it would be to say that he was right, in what he'd written: that I was easy compared to my mum.)

At the time he'd called 'convenient' he must have been watching from the window, because his front door opened as I raised my hand to knock.

'Oh,' he said, looking me up and down, 'it's you, is it? Well, come through, then. We're all out in the back.'

We? I thought. But he was already walking back down the dark hallway. I followed him in, pulled the door shut behind me. His hair was completely white now, almost blue-white, and cropped very short. It looked institutional. That was hard to take, for some reason. It frightened me. I could hear him breathing through his mouth, too, gasping in a sharp breath with every second step, as he walked before me, out into the garden, back out into the sun, where the 'we' turned out to be two boys busy building some kind of flat-pack shed, was it? It looked like a shed: three tongue-and-groove walls bending back crookedly from a small floor. The boys – both with their shiny, sky-blue football shirts off and tucked into the back pockets of their jeans – were leaning over an instruction sheet laid out on the picnic table. They looked to be eleven, twelve years old (although I can never tell what age children are). Their names were Steven and Simon.

'Speak up!' Dad said.

I didn't know how to look at them, as we were introduced like that. Not that we were really being introduced, of course. We were all being shown to each other.

'This is my smelly daughter,' Dad said. 'Now, I've told them about your book. They're under orders. What's it called?'

They didn't know.

'What's it called?' he said again. And then,

'Well, tell them. You'll remember that? Now, how's the second one coming along? Finished that yet?'

'Goodness, no,' I said.

'Having trouble?'

He grinned at the boys.

'Oh,' I said, 'only the usual, requisite amount of trouble, I think.'

Dad was smiling broadly now. He looked very happy.

'I want to go back to New York to finish it,' I said, 'ideally. I wrote the last one in New York, so . . .'

'Of course you did,' he said.

And then, turning back to the boys, 'She's having trouble,' he said. 'Well, a lot of people do. A lot of people only have one book in them. There are a lot of examples of that. It's quite common, actually. Now, you will say hello to Bunbury for me, won't you, in New York?'

'Bunbury?'

'Oh, have I caught her out there? You don't know who Bunbury is? Do *you* know who Bunbury is?' he said, addressing the smaller of the boys.

'I know who he is, I just don't know what you mean,' I said. I was trying to sound friendly,

41

but I really didn't know what he was implying. That I hadn't been to America? That I liked having time to myself?

'Oh, do you not?' he said.

He explained who Bunbury was to the boys, who stood blinking in the sun.

As we walked back inside, past the downstairs office (I saw the computer in there, humming on standby) and through to the kitchen, Dad spoke excitedly.

'Boys like these have nowhere to go on Saturdays, you know,' he said. 'And they really don't get exposed to *anything*. They were in here before, this morning, and they didn't even know what a Brazil nut was! "What's this, Brian?" they said. And I said, "Try one!"'

And then he was bustling about, running an ice tray under the tap, and then setting four pint glasses out on the surface, and popping the ice out into them.

I remembered those glasses, the feel of them – dunked in hot water, slippy with bubbles – as I had to wash them up three times, four times. 'Again,' Dad would say, pointing at the sink, the cracked saucer with the steaming scouring pad on it. And then, standing beside me: 'Show me. Call that clean?'

'I'm training you up!' he used to say. (And it always was me, never Liam.)

Now he was pouring out Coke from a huge bottle. The ice cubes were cracking.

What else did I remember from those half-terms? Not too much. I remembered the bunk beds. I remembered for breakfast we'd have our choice from a Kellogg's Variety Pack. Dad always bought one of those for each of us, and one for himself, too: eight small, individual boxes of cereal. Liam and I would as a rule eat the Coco Pops first, on that first Saturday morning, and then by the last day would be left with something which I think was called Start or Go, which was very unpleasant, somehow chewy and spongy at the same time. It made the milk taste of malt. Dad ate his in the same order, too, I think. Coco Pops first. I don't remember what we did all day. I remember eating Marks and Spencer sandwiches on a bench in Kew Gardens once. They were nice. I thought about them afterwards. And there was a trip to see a children's play called *The Gingerbread Man* and once we went to a swimming pool (in Richmond, was it?) with water slides and a wave machine whose turning-on was heralded by a loud siren and a countdown on an electronic board: a cascade of orange dots

spelling out, THREE! TWO! ONE! TSUNAMI!
I remember we had to have a bath every morning
(at home it was Wednesday and Sunday nights).
So there was the motoring chug of the taps and
the landing would fill with steam. (That's how I
remember it, anyway. Clouds of steam and the
smell of Badedas.) And then, again there'd be,
'Call that clean?' and, 'Again!' and, 'Arms up,
now!' Did Liam get that, too? I expect he did,
but I never asked. We didn't talk to each other
too much.

'Well, you don't look like a vegetarian!' Dad
said now.

'I'm a vegan,' I said, turning around. 'But what
do you mean?'

'I'm not complaining! Oh, there it is. Pouting!
I've been looking forward to that. Don't be so
sensitive.' He was chuckling. 'I'm paying you a
compliment.'

Opening the fridge again, he stooped to peer
into it, before reaching in and taking out a lemon.

'Fish is okay, I presume?' he said.

'Pardon me?' I said.

But he just looked at me.

'For me to eat?' I said. 'No, it's not.'

He kept looking at me. After a moment, he
said it again: 'Fish is okay, I presume?'

I shook my head. I still wasn't sure if he was joking.

'Well, no,' I said. And then, 'Clue's in the word vegan.'

His eyes widened at that. Just the tiniest bit. He was still breathing through his mouth.

'I did tell you,' I said.

But now he just harrumphed. He looked wounded. He was wearing a white, Mao-collared shirt and rolled-up, khaki trousers, and flip-flops. His ankles looked swollen, purple in places, grey in others. His heels looked like old potatoes.

'Well, I don't know what else you can eat,' he said.

Now it was my turn not to say anything. I felt too cruel, though. So I smiled, and shrugged. 'Well . . .'

'Cheese?'

'No, I don't eat cheese.'

He kept on peering glumly into the fridge.

'Oh, Dad, I did say. And you know I don't eat meat. I haven't eaten meat in fifteen years.'

What I didn't say here, but almost said, was, *I ate chicken once, when you tricked me, and you and Liam laughed at me.* But I didn't like the note that sounded. I didn't even like the note it sounded when I thought it. And anyway, I'd always only felt sorry for him about that incident, remembering him chuckling away with Liam (who I think was six), and saying, 'Looks like she's enjoying that, doesn't she?'

'Well, don't worry about it,' I said. 'I can have beans on toast or something.'

He straightened up, and closed the fridge door. 'Haven't got beans,' he said.

Back over at the chopping board, he sliced up the lemon, sliding a thick wedge onto the rim of each glass. Again we were both looking out of the open window at the boys in the garden. They'd stopped working for now, instead they were talking, and then the taller of the two wiped his forehead with his shirt and then looked at his watch.

'So I had Radio 3 on in here earlier,' Dad said, shaking his head, 'and it was Verdi's Requiem, you remember that?'

I'm afraid I didn't, really, but I nodded. He went on, 'Well, again, it was, "What's this, Brian?" Never heard anything *like* it! So I just said, "It's Joe Green! Giuseppe Verdi – Italian for Joe Green!" Really keen, you know: "Can I borrow that, Brian?" Ask them, when we go out,' he said, nodding at me, eyes wide, curator of the world again. 'Just ask them,' he said. 'Joe Green.'

So I nodded too, again, and smiled, and then looked back out into the garden, and had a sip of my Coke. Dad appeared out there soon enough, stepping carefully with his tray, and grimacing as he bent to set it down on the table. And then he was off again: walking around the half-built shed, looking it over. The boys picked up their drinks and held them in front of their slick chests. Squinting at the high sun, they yawned one by one. They seemed to pass the same pleasant, summer's day yawn back and forth between them, until Dad started talking to them more directly, again widening his eyes and thrusting his large, white-haired head forward. As he went on, one hand in his pocket now, apparently asking each of them questions they didn't have answers for, I saw all the ease and naturalness leave those boys. Suddenly they were standing very still, and with that expression on their faces again – or rather, that absence of an expression.

Back at home that evening, I covered my computer keyboard with a newspaper as I had Cathy type and then retype a new password for my email account. Neither of us knew what it was, so that lock was glued. Whether my dad continued to expend himself in there, I don't know; from one oubliette to another ('*Am I alone?*'). I'd like to think that he didn't but perhaps that's very pious of me, if that's what he wanted to do. Perhaps now I'm the one being like that.

It was four years before I heard anything else from him. I was back in New York then, just for three months, trying to start another book. As I've said, I used to like to go to America to write. I could think, I found, over there. What in England were cankers, in America became golden apples. (They really did, those first few times. Strange to think of that now.) I was subletting a studio on Avenue B this time. A tea-caddy-sized place, it harboured a stewed, spicy-smelling, liquor-like darkness, even as high summer confounded the streets. Even as the streets smelled scorched. I'd been up all night trying miserably to get something down, sitting cramped at the fold-down kitchen table with the A/C wheezing at me, when I got a message from Cathy. She'd sent on a link, with the subject line, *Uh Oh!* I don't know what I was expecting, when I clicked through to my own Wikipedia page, but this is what I got (it's still cached on that site):

Aislinn Kelly is an English novelist, born in London in 1977. She now lives in Manchester. Her first novel; *The Universe* was published when she was 22 years old. Since then she has published 2 more, *Sanctum, Sputum* and *Abominable Houseguest* (2005). *The Universe* was quite poetical, but since then it has been downhill. A book of short stories lies buried in this history. It was A totally inconsequential effort.

The critics gave her some breathing space with her 'difficult' second 'novel', *Sanctum, Sputum* (2002). But in every detail this was biographical: A collection of bitter memories, and offences against her, by her close family. It's most central themes were vicious personal attacks by Aislinn on close family members. Not one single character in this rant is given any kind of positive image, not even a hint of one. The onset of paranoia was clear.

Abominable Houseguest continues were *Sanctum, Sputum* left off. The first half is again essentially a very childish rant against her mother, father, and one set of grandparents. All are seen as responsible for her extreme insecurity. Her total inability to see anything positive suggests the world she lives in as a terrifying place!

All interviews with 'Ms' Kelly mention her 'pout'. The expression on her face when she was born was described as an aggressive curiosity, but on reflection, a pout may have been more accurate! The attitude thus reflected has reached a crescendo in recent years!

An excuse often offered by her is that she is an 'artiste' and this is how 'artistes' behave. I hope she grows up, but at 27 years old, it is probably too late. The fear is that the paranoia is now firmly established!

Without thinking, I started writing back: *Fuck! Well, at least he didn't 'put' 'second' 'in' 'quotes'. He gave me that. Ha ha.*

Horrible. I tried again: *I have *never* slagged off my grandparents.*

Which was true. But I didn't send that either. I didn't reply.

5

I have wondered why my mum didn't stop me. As the years passed, I mean, until I was twenty-nine years old, and still so often steering our conversations to the same tense impasse, where I'd say, with unvarying incredulity, that I couldn't imagine carrying on if I'd found myself in her position: trapped, and powerless, and obliterated in that kind of marriage, for *seven years* . . . When it showed in my eyes, and the way I leaned forward, my sickly thrall to that queer compact: my origin, she should have stopped me, I thought, looking back. (Well, shouldn't she?) But she'd only said, 'Well, no, dear. Suicide isn't everyone's first recourse in a crisis, believe it or not! Anyway, I had you two kiddies, didn't I? You were my priority.'

She had another word for herself: 'Oh, yes, I'm *indomitable.* Your grandma always said that to me, too, you know, from when I was very small. They both did. And then when I was a teenager, I'd just be sitting there and one of them would say, "She's not fazed by anything. Look at her." And I wasn't really.'

Wasn't she, though?

'No. Never. And I was older than you when I had to move back in with them, too. And I had nothing, then. Absolutely nothing. *No* job, *no* money, *two* kiddies; living in that box room after having my own flat in London. God, I felt sick every morning. Just so nauseous, having to face another day. But I did it.'

That box room: the low camp bed and the clothes rail, the Stack'n'Store baskets and the thick curtains, letting the light in in pinpricks. I always thought I'd learned to read in there, cloistered away, but my dates were all off, as it turned out.

'No, this was in Acton. I took this. That's not your grandma's house, is it? No, I know because it was the day before your second birthday, and we'd been out that afternoon to buy you a little cake. You'd picked one out. I went to get the camera from the living room, because you looked so sweet with your hair sticking up, don't you? Ah . . . poor little thing. But *then*, when I came back, I heard you were reading out your bedtime book for yourself, oh, ever so fast. And I didn't want to interrupt you, so I waited in the hall, and when you'd finished, I came in and said, "Well done, Aislinn!" And you held the book in the air with one hand, and your little teddy in the air with the other . . .'

Yes, I remembered that part. I felt very exhilarated. Also, I had a strong desire – after I'd enjoyed that moment – to read another book through, and then hold that up in the air.

'But you *can't* remember,' Mum said, 'you were tiny!'

I was small. But – I remembered all sorts. I remembered that man Derek, who moved in with us later; his black TR7 parked up outside, and his silly, shaggy haircut. I used to bring him up with Mum when I was feeling bilious.

'Oh, are you still going on about that?' she said. 'Why are you so obsessed?'

That wasn't hard to explain.

'Not *beat*,' she said. 'Oh, you'd see a man hang, wouldn't you? Beat. No, *hit* when you were naughty.'

We were seven and five, is what we were. Did she have any thoughts on that?

'Well, I was distraught, yes,' she said, 'very distressed, of course.'

She was a strange woman. I didn't say that to

53

her to insult her. I was surprised she took it in, to be honest. But she did, and then her expression really curdled.

'Don't you dare say that,' she said. 'Don't you dare. *You're* the one. *You.* You're not around normal people enough to know what normal is!'

True enough. I did lead an isolated life.

I lead a very lonely and isolated life, and I called it — decorum. Every year she'd say, 'Any plans for Christmas?'

Three years ago, I finally snapped: 'No I haven't. That's ten years now, in quarantine,' I said. 'Thanks for asking.'

Did she hear me? Did I deserve to be heard? Perhaps not. We were in a café in the Northern Quarter, a fairy-lit, under-heated cove and us the only customers, eating so early. Behind the twinkling prow of the bar at the back of the room, I could see the young waitress standing and licking her teeth, along with the owner who'd greeted us so heartily earlier. She was now looking rather mirthless as she stared down at her phone. Mum was probably aware of them, too. Perhaps she saw their reflection in the dripping window behind me.

'Well,' she said, 'Liam's going to your dad's on Boxing Day.'

'Oh. Right. I didn't know they were in touch.'

'Well, they weren't,' she said, 'were they? But Liam was desperate for tickets to the United Arsenal match, and your uncle Joe works there now, doesn't he? So Liam rang your dad up, and your dad rang Joe up and somehow got two tickets, and in return, he's going to go for a meal there afterwards.'

'Wow. Well, tell him to be careful.'

'Hm?'

'Sounds like a bit of a Faustian pact to me.'

'Oh no. I think Liam's wise enough to your father not to be affected by all that. He knows to just ignore him.'

'Lucky him.'

Again, 'Hm?'

'I'm just saying, the man's unbalanced. Having to deal with him all my life made me really ill, in case you hadn't noticed. It fucks you up being around that kind of a black hole.'

'Er, excuse me, yes, I was *married* to him, you know. I know he's not the ideal partner!'

'What are you talking about, "partner"?'

'Oh, you know what I mean.'

'Not really. Listen, can you at least ask Liam not to tell him anything about me?'

'Like what?'

'Like anything. Anything about my life. Where I'm living. I don't want to get stalked again.'

'Well, what's Liam going to tell him? Do you think everyone sits around discussing *you*? Er . . . sorry to disillusion you!'

'Jesus. Okay.'

I can usually anticipate an attack of asperity. When I get that imp in me, I tend to take a breath, and decide whether or not to go through with it. And then I go through with it, usually without too much gusto, in the event. As now – I put down my wine glass, and leaned back in my spindly metal chair before saying, 'It is quite unfair, though, isn't it? Don't you think? He's totally fine, getting his football tickets; you're totally fine, *obviously*; meanwhile, look at me. I mean, why do you think that is? That I get to suffer? And you're all so blithe, so fucking delighted all the time. Why has it all devolved to me? Every reverse, squared. Is it my face, do you think? Is that what gets you people wound up so tight? This face?'

These were all serious questions, believe me.

The face across the table didn't seem to register that I was speaking, though. She appeared to be chewing her food, but I'd seen her put an empty fork into her mouth. Her plate had been clean for a while. So then I watched her swallow nothing. There were the oval frames of her spectacles, there was her lipstick. And then her magenta mouth, her yellow and grey teeth, said: 'Well, maybe you just got more of his genes than my genes.'

After a very lonely moment, I asked her what *that* meant.

'Well,' she said brightly, 'because he's "fucked up", and you're "fucked up".'

Again, she wasn't looking at me when she said that. Even as she used my own words. The worst thing was, I knew she believed it now, too, having said it. She'd heard herself say it, it had struck her as logical, and now she believed it.

'That's a horrible thing to say,' I said.

Again she smiled blandly. She said nothing.

'And – you don't care.'

Still smiling, her eyes fixed on some point in the middle distance.

'Of course we care,' she said, 'we *always* want you to come for Christmas.'

'Right,' I said, and then I watched her take the green paper napkin from her lap and fold it up, and set it on her plate; she held it bunched there as she craned her neck around, looking for someone to ask for the bill.

★

That 'we' was her and her new husband, I presumed. Or her and Liam? That was possible, too. Maybe she meant the three of them.

She'd married again two years ago (after Liam had finally moved out), to Howard, a history teacher she'd met in one of her groups. At the wedding, he'd been very personable, kissing everyone's cheeks in the continental style, and then, all evening, he'd deployed an entertaining repertoire of funny voices: an Irish peasant savant, a smooth jazz hound, a soused aristocrat.

'Nao-ow,' he'd said, stretching out the syllable's creaking, and waggling his fingers, and widening his shot, swagged eyes, 'let us all strip naked! And dance — like satyrs!'

At the reception he was Paul McCartney, bobbing about the table, and appearing in all of the photographs, with pursed lips and two thumbs up. Those pictures showed Mum looking much as she always looked: unreadable, and my drunk brother, his face flushed and slick, leering at his new stepdad's larking about. (You didn't think I'd let anyone take a picture of me, did you?)

I'd seen Howard only a couple of times since then, when I'd been over to visit Mum. He'd used the same voices. When he wasn't talking like that, he sat with one hand gripping and covering his face. He'd sat there on the kitchen chair like that, set like a cairn. He was a short man: quite plump and high-cheeked. His chin-length hair was still nearly black, though his bushy beard was white. What else did I know about him? Oh yes, Mum said he hadn't made a will, because he was 'superstitious'.

'We're bohemians!' she'd taken to declaring. They went on a lot of city breaks together. I hated to hear about them. I hated to look at the endless photographs of the meals they were about to eat, their grinning faces looming in turn over full plates. I had to turn my head away.

'You're so rude,' she'd say. 'Why are you so bloody rude?'

Once I came out and said it: 'Because you terrify me, and I can't stand it.'

'Well then,' she said, 'then you must just *pretend* to be interested, like a normal, civilised grown-up. Anyway, you should be interested. We're interesting people. We do interesting things!'

The next time we spoke – a couple of years ago, this, I was still between books – she had other concerns. We were sitting in the kitchen in Howard's house in Mossley Hill (she'd moved in after they married), under the auspices of one of his paintings: a large portrait of Charles

Baudelaire. I'd only gone there because I was desperate.

'No, you listen,' Mum said, 'what I'm more worried about is you setting yourself on fire with those candles. Now have you got a smoke alarm? Just tell me, just, okay, well, have you tested it? Because you *must* test it regularly. You don't want to die like that, what a tragedy. Just tell me.'

She slapped her hand on the table and looked exasperated, or about to laugh, I thought, was she?

'Oh, bugger off,' I said.

'Well, no, *you* bugger off,' she said. 'You're so rude!'

I just needed some money. She had plenty, since Grandma died.

'Oh, I'm getting *old* now, Aislinn,' she said. 'I can't keep helping you. I mean, how do you manage when you're away? You're supposed to be a sophisticated young woman, now, aren't you? I mean, do you behave like this when you're in New York? How do you manage? Do you speak to people in New York like this? You just seem to lurch from one crisis to the next, don't you?'

Well, I disagreed with that. It was the same crisis. Ongoing. And one that was mysteriously not often a pressing issue when I was 'away'.

'Well, time to grow up,' Mum said. 'Other

people manage. That's what people do. I mean, you're like a black hole. It's take take take. What about me, hey?'

'What about you? We're not talking about you. I'm in trouble here. I'm trying to work and I can't eat, and you're shouting at me!'

'Well, what do you expect me to say? Oh, *well done*. Oh, congratulations, *what* a clever girl, having no money.'

She was stroking my arm deliriously as she said this: her pitch at a pantomime of maternal pride. I didn't like that. I pulled away. Still – she was going to give me the money, I guessed, so that was one problem solved. Not that there weren't other problems.

'Well, I won't be here forever, you know,' Mum said, 'Aislinn. And then what will you do? I mean . . . Well, it's better to face facts, isn't it? Why are *you* so upset? *I'm* not frightened. I mean, you saw Grandma, didn't you?'

I had seen Grandma. She'd looked – deflated. They'd put her in a dreadful nightie. I'd touched her, too, on the neck, behind her downy earlobe, now as dry as old pastry. And no, it wasn't frightening, or even particularly solemn. It wasn't anything. Mum had said the same.

'Oh no, I didn't feel anything,' she said. 'No, nothing. Not with either of them.'

She'd guessed Grandma was dead when she hadn't shown up for lunch that Sunday; when I came back from the bus stop alone. 'Oh dear, poor Grandma,' she'd said, and then she'd closed her eyes while she thought what to do. I remember her walking past me out to the car in her slippers, and then she came back in to turn off the hob.

Grandma often came on Sundays after Grandpa died. I don't think she was feeding herself very well back then. I know that when I visited her towards the end it was best not to walk past the kitchen when she was making tea, for risk of seeing her briskly scraping the mould from whatever you were about to eat. There was always something on the turn in that fridge: tubs of left-overs were stacked up in there for weeks on end; baked beans hardened to pellets, fruit purée starting to fizz, tinned plum tomatoes topped with frosted islands of green mould.

Grandma had come on holiday with us, too, that last summer. Two weeks to Barcelona, she paid for all of us. I remember the dry swish of her crêpe-y trouser-suits: loose trousers, a camisole and a short-sleeved jacket all in the same pale hue – lavender, or apricot, or eau-de-Nil. 'Cruise wear' she called these outfits, these 'get-ups', as she turned in front of the mirror in the cool hotel foyer. Every day, lunch was a quest for a toastie. Liam got fed up with that, and soon he was rolling his eyes and saying, 'Ooh, a toastie!' in satiric imitation of her, and then, as we looked over another menu outside another café: 'For fuck's sake,' he'd say. At last we'd sit outside some-where and Grandma would fan herself with her guidebook. Her sunglasses' lenses were large, smoky, octagonal. She'd curl her lip at Liam and turn her head away. The books she gave me to read were by Betty MacDonald and Stella Gibbons. She looked like an older version of the author photo of Betty MacDonald, I thought, on the back of that Penguin book. She still wore her hair that way, anyway, fixing it in pin curls every night, in the room we shared, twisting it and gripping it – her large head would bristle with grips – before rubbing in her face cream and then her thick hand cream.

'Oh, it is cruel,' she said one night, 'how once you can afford nice jewellery, your hands look like this. I remember my Nana Jessop saying that to me, too.'

'I mean, look at that,' she said, spreading her

63

fingers. Her skin was baggy, the veins like old lead pipes.

'Oh, I didn't get close enough for that,' Mum said. 'Yuck. Mind you, she always used to say that, "She never hugs me." I couldn't bear to, though. Do you remember those squishy forearms? And that stomach? When I was tiny I used to say that to her: "Why are you so fat?" Aren't kids horrible, hey? And then she'd say, "I had *you* in there, Tarly." Ugh. I'd feel sick.'

'Tarly.' That was how she'd pronounced her own name when she was first learning to talk.

Now this was my mother's voice: '. . . another thing your grandma always said: "Whatever makes you happy." Why's everyone so obsessed with that? I've never understood it. But anyway, just to pee them off, I'd always say, "I will be happy as long as I'm with *Anthony*." And then your grandma's face would just freeze. You know how she was. And then she'd go out of the room, and send your grandpa in to have a word, and he'd say, "Now listen, you must promise us you won't marry that Anthony. Please promise us. Just promise." Now, I didn't want to marry anyone, yuck, but I *wouldn't* promise . . .

'I don't think it ever occurred to me to aim for *happiness*, though. I mean, do you do that? No, just try to get through with as little pain as possible, that's the way . . .'

And deeper into the past: I was small, and in sobs over a poem. When she reached for my book, I grabbed it back, making myself ugly.

'Good grief, what's wrong with you now?' she said.

And then, having moved some old papers and sat down next to me on the stairs, she said, 'Oh dear, look at that miserable face. Just *look* at that *sullen*, miserable face.'

She had her back straight, her hands clasped in her lap.

Well, my hot animal state seemed grisly to me, too. The way I was breathing, which sounded like a drone. It was that thing I'd copied out: 'And I Always Thought' by Brecht. Every time I read it this happened, I experienced this high distress. I would keep on reading it, though. It was a strange game I'd devised. I knew it was.

'Aislinn?' Mum said.

But I was holding onto a banister now, and pressing my face against that, and waiting for her to go away.

As she stood up, she said: 'Well, I don't *want* you in the living room with a face like that, anyway, I don't think, do I? No, I don't *want* you in there looking like that, ruining the atmosphere. Oh no, you *should* sit out here on your own while I sit in the warm. Yes, *whatever you do* don't come in the living room, and warm up, and watch TV with your mum . . .'

A later tack of hers was to try to be 'practical' when I couldn't stop crying.

'Well, I'm a practical person,' she said, 'aren't I? That's my job. That's what I do all day. Problem-solve.'

She used to use a shirt back, from one of mine or Liam's school shirts, or sometimes she'd pull the cardboard strip from a packet of KitKats and use that, drawing a line down the middle of it first, and then she'd head the columns: *Problems* and *Solutions*. Or sometimes she'd write, *Course of Action!*

'Now, dear me, what's the matter?' she'd say. And, 'Calm down, Ash. I'll get a KitKat card.'

The first time, I was seven or eight, and I told her that I didn't have any friends.

NO FRIENDS, she wrote down.

'I feel very lonely,' I said.

'Well, that comes under the same heading, I think,' she said, 'doesn't it, as "no friends"?'

'I don't think I exist,' I said. 'I'm frightened all the time. Nobody ever looks at me or talks to me.'

'Oh, one thing at a time. What do you mean you don't think you exist? What does that mean? Oh, you exist all right! I think we can all testify to *that*.'

An analogue, I think: a few years later, she was refusing to buy Liam a video game he wanted, and he kicked up a real fuss, attacking her for hours with his usual scornful teenage largesse; the most disgusted incomprehension, really, at this outraged droit de seigneur. He followed her from room to room, jeering. He stood over her while she ate her tea. (She was eating, as usual, alone in the back room, off a tray on the foot-stool.) Hating him for it, I knelt down by his bed that night and hissed at him: Did he know what she earned, I asked, because *I* did, *I*'d found out . . .

It didn't work, though. The next morning, he stood in the kitchen doorway, red-eyed and indignant, and demanding, even as his bottom lip wobbled: 'Are we poor, or what?

'Well?' he said. 'I've got a right to know!'

And then he took a step forward, saying, '*Are . . . we . . . poor?*'

And, 'What the fuck is this, hey?'

Walking around her now, and looking her up and down: 'Can you not answer a simple question,' he said, '*you dumb cow?*'

6

Ginger tea is what she used to drink in the
mornings, first thing, carrying her mug back
upstairs with her at five past six, and one for me,
too, if I was awake. (Liam was never awake.) She
left the mug on my window sill. I always thought
she liked the taste of it. I did: the heat, the
pungency, the way that tickled your nose. For
years, for Christmas and for her birthday, I always
bought her tins of ginger biscuits or tubs of
crystallised ginger sweets because I thought she
liked the taste. I'd get her other things, too, but
always something ginger flavoured. Last year was
when she called a halt, when I sent her some
ginger-scented bath foam. Not that she didn't
like it, exactly.

'Well, ginger's supposed to suppress nausea,
isn't it?' she said. 'That's why I used to drink that
tea. Because I used to feel so sick. I'd just feel
so sick every morning about how my life was. I
didn't want to be in work feeling sick, did I?'

That's quite a funny story, I think, in a way.

And here's another one: a couple of days after that visit when I was asking for the cash, I received this:

Caroline Tully *Various*

Aislinn,

As requested I have put £500 into your account – it should have cleared by the time you read this.

As I said on Saturday, you are almost thirty and I am retiring soon so this will be the last time I will ever bail you out. You say you earned 5k last year – surely you see that having tried to make a living from writing for nine years, you cannot survive and having achieved some of your goals, it is now time to stop.

*You will have to take **any** kind of job – difficult I know in the current climate but the DWP and HMRC are taking on loads of people to cope with all the current redundancies – try there? Having a daily routine and mixing with other people instead of working at home on your own will broaden your perspective on life and take you away from endless introspection and obsessing over your childhood. Your present regime seems to me just a retreat from your real*

70

problems of penury and mental illness. Surely you knew, given your financial circumstances, that your latest trip to New York was a mistake?

What exactly were the terrible things in your childhood that have 'ruined' your life? My so-called 'smirk' the other night was actually a look of total bewilderment. No one's childhood is ideal but most people grow up, make a life of their own as best they can and 'move on'. I know the divorce and leaving London must have been traumatic but you had a mother and grandma who cared for you.

I worked hard at a full-time, stressful job to give you a house in a pleasant area, and as much attention as I could. This is beyond the dreams of most children. In return you marred most of our weekends and holidays with your unfathomable behaviour, vandalised my belongings and furniture and fittings, didn't invite me to your graduation, screamed obscenities at me in the street, make it necessary for me to walk on eggshells every time we meet, and have treated me in a rude, disrespectful and hurtful manner for as long as I can remember with no sign of remorse, in fact quite the opposite – a positively gleeful sadistic smile.

I am curious about your therapy. Did your GP refer you? What kind of therapy is it? How long will you be going? What outcomes is it working *towards? Is it on the NHS? I hope it is not entirely focused on your childhood.*

I am seriously worried that you are obviously very ill with depression and depressed people have a wholly unbalanced view of themselves and other people – won't they give you any medication? It would give you a break from the constant turmoil in your head and let you see the world differently. Keep asking for it. Ask and ask again. Howard says they will fob you off if they can.

You say 'I'm supposed to be your mum' – well, you are supposed to be my daughter – act like one – you show me scant consideration – even a Mother's Day text seems to be beyond you.

Aislinn, it really is time for a new start.

You are, of course, still welcome here for Christmas.

Mum xxx

Everything was funny. It had taken Cathy to point out to me that this email from my dad had been quite funny, too:

*There's nothing in it for **you** if I die!*

'No, not much!' she said.

A neat quip – I acknowledged that – but still,

a meaningless one, really. His being alive wasn't the problem. Just so long as he stopped pestering me. That was all I wanted. But then again, I didn't suppose I'd know one way or another how it would affect me, his really being gone, until it happened. Maybe that really would be the day. I talked to Mum about that, one evening last year.

'Oh no, well – you mustn't wait on *that*,' she said.

'I'm not,' I said. 'That's what I just said.'

'Because you know what your grandma used to say: *The devil's never in a hurry to take those he's sure of.*'

I shook my head. I didn't know where she got this stuff from.

'Then again, he'll be retiring in a few months, won't he?' she said. 'So maybe he'll just drop dead. Unmarried men do that. *Or* maybe he'll get dementia and you'll have to move in and look after him!'

'Oh thanks, Mum,' I said.

As it happened, I was with my dad when he heard his father had died. It was on one of those Saturdays towards the end, when I was picked up alone from the bottom of our street. We'd been round at Niall's house all afternoon, but it wasn't until the evening that he mentioned it. He was standing up by the hob then, cooking our tea, and Dad and I were sitting at his kitchen table with our pint glasses of Coke.

'Oh, er, our old man died last week,' Niall said.

'Oh. Right,' Dad said.

'Buried Wednesday. Gerry saw to it.'

Dad pursed his lips and shrugged, although Niall's back was turned to him.

'Yeah, these are done now,' Niall said.

'Well, *anyway*, speaking of miserable old men, where's Howard? Can you go and tell him we're—'

But Howard was already coming through the kitchen door, eyes wide, left arm raised in greeting.

'I am not *late*!' he said. 'I am on *time*!'

I started to visit those two last September. I'd stayed away for such a long time, and then even when I wanted to visit I couldn't, in case I ran into Liam, who seemed to be round there a lot. It was after he moved down to London that I began to take the train over to Liverpool every few months, and I usually had an okay time. It depended on what kind of a mood I was in, really. (I mean, of course it did.) Anyway, I kept at it.

And I can't deny this: the first few times I went there, their house did look to me like just the kind of place I might have liked to grow up. It was peaceful, and clean. It was quiet. In the living room books were shelved floor to ceiling either side of the chimney breast, and there were paintings stacked on the other, blistery, dark red walls. In the fireplace a collection of votive candles looked like a spotted set of old organ pipes, and although there was a TV, the set they had back then was tiny and not often switched on. It was so old it didn't have a remote.

'Interactive!' Howard said.

He never watched the TV. Mum turned it on after tea some nights, but Howard was in the front room then, anyway. Sometimes he was reading, Mum told me, books about World War Two, nothing else, but just as often he liked to just sit in the dark.

'Well, fair enough,' I said, and Mum nodded and smiled pleasantly.

'Oh, but it's much better than when he first retired,' she said. 'He didn't take his dressing gown off for months, then! I used to get in from work and he'd be sitting in the corner of the settee in there, *exactly* where he'd been when I left. I was worried he was going to just slip down the side of the cushion. Poor thing. Ah. It'll be better when I retire. One more year to go!'

Here she rubbed her hands together.

'Can't *wait*!' she said.

I didn't have a TV myself so I didn't mind having it on. I liked it if a film came on, and Mum and I could sit and watch it.

Their kitchen always smelled nice, too. They took turns cooking, and seldom ate meat, and there was always a bottle of wine or bottles of beer on the table. The difficult thing, when I first started to go round there and sit with them, was that I often couldn't think of anything to say. So Howard would chew and chew, his eyes wide, and Mum would cut her food up into very small pieces before she ate it, and I'd eat too fast, and then decide to slow down, all the while racking my brain for a topic of conversation. Those two rarely talked to each other when I was there – or not in their own voices anyway, because she'd started speaking in tongues, too, at some point. She made her non sequiturs as Joyce Grenfell or Irene Handl, and he didn't respond, just kept chewing – and meanwhile I couldn't talk to them about my writing, or my love life, so – what did people discuss? I'd always end up talking about a film I'd seen, that Mum had seen or, more often, had wanted to see. (Howard flat out refused to go to the pictures with her. 'It's all *shite*, darling,' he said, so she went on her own after work every Monday.) The trouble then was that I often started over-compensating and blustering, just for the sake of sounding animated, and then Mum would look at me shyly and sometimes tut and shake her head. She always poured her beer out into a tiny glass, a commemorative glass for the Cambridge Real Ale Festival, which looked like it held about a quarter of a pint.

'Come for a walk with me and your mother tomorrow!' Howard said one night. 'Get some country air!'

I shrugged. 'I don't know. I'm not much for the countryside.'

'Well, yes, *I* used to feel like that,' he said, and then, after a moment, and squinting up at a corner of the ceiling: 'Max *Beerbohm* once said . . . that living in England is like *living in a lettuce*!'

Mum raised her eyebrows and smiled pleasantly at that, and ate another small mouthful.

When Howard got the black dog these days,

as well as his walks on Sundays, he would eat a square of dark chocolate. There was always a large bar of it ready on top of the bread bin, a thin ingot in embossed gold foil. Mum told me he'd last been seriously depressed about fifteen years ago, but then he'd taken just one Prozac pill and it had changed his outlook completely.

'It just reset him apparently,' she said. 'That was all it took. So – don't dismiss it out of hand, will you? Ash?'

She'd shown me a photograph of him back then, when he was still teaching at the local comprehensive. The picture must have been taken in the staff room: he was sitting on a low armchair and there was some piebald blue tinsel Sellotaped around the noticeboard behind him.

'Ah, he looks about twelve, doesn't he?' Mum said. 'Poor thing. I'm just saying, Howard, you look about twelve here! That looks like a *false* beard!'

'Yes!' Howard said.

Incidentally, there was one other occupant of that house by then, resident, incumbent, for the past few months: Howard's tuba, which had appeared in February. His two daughters, remembering a yen he'd expressed long ago – decades ago, so far as I could tell – to learn to play the theme tune from *Hancock's Half Hour*, had clubbed together and bought it him for Christmas, along with a short course of beginner's lessons. All he had to do was go and collect it from a music shop in Manchester; but as Mum told me when I was round there at the end of January, he kept putting it off.

'Oh, he's furious!' she said.

Howard, who was sitting at the kitchen table, lifted his head from his hands then.

'Yes, be careful what you wish for, Aislinn,' he said, darkly. 'Be careful what you *say* . . .'

Things had changed by the next time I called, though. I could hear him in the background, practising.

'What is that tune?' I said. 'Is it "Love Me Do"?'

'No, I think that's . . . Oh, I don't know, is it "We Wish You a Merry Christmas"?'

'I don't think so,' I said.

'Oh, he loves it, though,' Mum said. 'I can't prise him off it. First thing in the morning until last thing at night.'

'I'm a tuba widow!' she said.

And later: 'We went to Bath the week before last, just for three days, and he said he was missing it terribly. Couldn't *wait* to get back to it. He took the mouthpiece — whatever you call it — with him, in his pocket!'

'Like a dummy,' I said.

'Yes!' Mum said. And then, 'Oh . . . now, don't be cruel, Aislinn.'

I told Mum I was thinking about going to America again. In the past I hadn't told her until I'd got back. I'd answered the phone to her over there and pretended I was in my flat, many times.

'Oh. Well — can you afford that?' she said.

We were in her kitchen, still sitting at the table after dinner.

'Just about,' I said. 'I can go for the summer. I want to try to start work again, and therapy finishes next month so I am free to go. Although — that's going to be strange.'

'Well, where will you go? To New York? You can't afford that.'

'No — somewhere else. I don't know yet.'

'Well, do you know anyone there?'

'I'm not going to socialise.'

'No, I know that, but — what's the point, then? What will you do?'

'I don't know. Be peaceful. It's hard for me to think here.'

'Well – can't you be peaceful in your own flat?'

'Pffft.'

'What does that mean?'

'I need space to think.'

'And you don't have any money. Where is this money coming from, Aislinn? You need to think about getting a job. I mean, don't look to me.'

'I'm not. I can afford to go.'

'What about the spare room here? That's quiet. That's got a little desk in it.'

'Oh, no thanks.'

'That's a lovely little room! What do you mean, no thanks?'

'Oh, come on.'

'You *can't* just keep going away, Aislinn.'

'Oh, can't I?' I said.

And then: 'You know, I haven't been away in years, actually. You know that. I've been stuck here. Moving into the sensory-deprivation room won't help me. I'm trying to go forwards.'

'And you *must* take care about money,' Mum said. 'I can't bail you out again. That was a *one-time thing*. I retire in November and that's *that*.'

'I know. Thank you.'

'I just – I don't know. I wouldn't like to go somewhere where I didn't know anybody. Don't you get terribly lonely?'

'Is that a *joke*?' I said.

But then she went shy again, she seemed to smile out of awkwardness, she sort of smiled over my shoulder.

'Okay. Well . . . Okay. I'm sure you know what you're doing, love,' she said.

II

II

Leaving, as always, only felt like passing through a series of airlocks. I kept myself awake with coffee and was gradually drained of pep, exiting this time after fifteen hours, in a not unpleasant daze, through the smoked-glass sliding doors of Concourse B, Indianapolis Airport. The afternoon that met me was dazzling, and hairdryer hot; the air parched and syrupy with diesel.

The landscape looked unreal at first. Through the tinted windows of the IndyGo ShuttleBus the huge sky was smogged to a kitsch-y turquoise, and the boundless cornfields, too − their yellow looked a little blue, a little dusty. One dark red tractor beaded the horizon.

After twenty minutes: the outskirts of the city; a patchwork of empty lots. Here were scabby expanses of asphalt, moonscapes of white rubble. The heat haze pinched at the air out there, conjuring hot-spirit, clear-flame imps above the ashen dirt, among the billboard struts. Up ahead, downtown was a close pack of towers in bronze and cobalt mirrored glass, echoing out the morning sun.

The address I had saved in my phone was another half an hour's taxi ride away, and proved to be a large, shabby white-frame house. A young woman was sitting on the steps of the porch as we drew up, holding her hair in her lap like a pet. Walking down the path to meet me, she squinted toothily. She wore pale denim shorts and a loose white shirt, neon green flip-flops. Shouldering my bag, I reached out my free hand to shake her hand.

'Hello there. Paula, is it?'

'Yes, hello!' she said. 'And you're Aislinn? Goodness. Hi there!'

Her ponytail fell to her waist: tawny brown and tatty. She took hold of it again as we went inside, winding it around her knuckles. In her other plump hand she was fidgeting at a set of keys.

As I followed her up the three flights of stairs to her place, she explained again how she'd already moved in with her boyfriend – he had a garden – but that she still had to see out her lease here. She hadn't in our emails, and didn't now, ask me what my business was. Instead, holding open her apartment door, she said, 'Okay. So, welcome, and come on in. You can put down that suitcase at last. That's all you brought?'

I nodded and smiled, dropped my bag and rested my case against the wall, and then I rolled my shoulders and stretched my arms out in front of me.

'Well,' she said, and again she shrugged and smiled, and pulled on her ponytail, tugging on it as if it were a bell rope.

'Oh, are you totally worn out?' she said.

I shook my head.

'I'll be fine,' I said, and then I yawned into my fist.

Together we walked around the two and a half attic rooms: a living room and kitchen and then a larger bedroom with a sloping roof and a skylight window. The place felt peaceful and clean. It smelled unlived-in, which I liked: a sort of wood-shaving-y, freshly hoovered smell. Throughout, the walls were painted a chalky turquoise-blue, and peppered with holes where pictures had been taken down. Paula had left me bedding and towels, and one set of crockery and cutlery (she opened a cupboard and then a drawer to show me).

'This all looks great, thank you,' I said.

She smiled at that, and then bit her bottom lip and shook her head. She could have been seventeen, or forty: the only lines on her moon-face appearing now in bunches under the corners of her eyes. I paid up front for the three months, and we regarded each other even more amiably then, over that chubby, pocket-hot fold of cash.

'Thank you,' I said, taking the keys.

'Oh, you're so welcome,' Paula said.

After she'd left I went to the kitchen to get myself a glass of water. The window by the sink overlooked the empty street, running straight for as far as I could see. The sun was high – a white torch in deep blue – and the tarmac glinted like an ocean.

2

It took me a while to register that my phone was ringing: even as I sat up, knowing that something had woken me; even as I was looking at the thing, blinking and jittering there on the floor.

Ewan, though. I hadn't thought of him for a long time. Not for years.

'Hello?' I said.

'Hello?' he said. And then, '. . . *hear* you?'

'Hello,' I said again.

'Oh, *hello*, darling! Yes, it's me here. London calling. Thought I'd try my luck, like. Hey, you're not *asleep*, are you?'

'I'm – half asleep,' I said. My mouth still didn't seem to be working, though. I worked my jaw, licked my teeth.

'Just lying there. *I* see. You sound asleep, to be honest. But, you know, doesn't hurt to *answer* your phone once in a while.'

'What for?'

'Is right,' he said. 'Hello?'

'Yes, hello. Just – give me a second.'

I got back under the covers then, the sheets and the blanket, and curled back up like I had been before. My eyes were watering. I was shivering.

'Ok,' I said, 'I'm ready. Go on. But where are you calling from anyway? What's happening? I think I am asleep. Hey, it sounds public.'

'Oh, no. I'm just at mine, like. That's the telly. I'll turn that off now. I just got home, actually, a little bit ago. Now the old sun's coming up. The old rain's coming down. And I thought about you.'

'You're in . . . Brixton?'

'Tufnell Park these days. Keep up. Keep up with me, darling, please.'

'Oh, right-ho. I used to live there.'

'Yes, I know you did, darling. Did you? Well, *I* like it here anyway. I was only in that other place because I was that poor. So so poor. The Terry Waite suite. I didn't even have a proper duvet there. I was sleeping in my clothes like a bum in a box! The old Irish pyjamas. Ha! You know, when you've grown up in a warm climate your blood gets thin. Turns into Diet *Pepsi*.'

'Hey now,' I said, 'Birkenhead's not a warm climate.'

'No, I know that, but we had central *heating*.

So . . . anyway. But you're not wearing any clothes now, though, are you?'

'Oh. No, I'm not.'

'No . . . Well, I'm the same like. Or I *will* be. This shirt has to go. Completely crumplestilt-skinned. So, yeah. I was thinking about you tonight, you know. I do miss you loads, actually.'

'Really.'

'Yeah . . . I miss Manchester.'

'I see.'

'No, I do, though.'

'Well, I believe you. But I'm not there any more, you know.'

'You're not there? Since when? I wasn't informed of this.'

'It's been ages now. Well, it's been a couple of weeks. I'm in America.'

'*No* . . .'

'I'm in Indianapolis.'

'Hey, make your mind up, darling!'

'Well – I am doing!'

'Okay, darling. Seriously, though?'

'Of course.'

'Okay. Well, sixty-seven pounds a minute here then.'

'Yes, it probably will cost you a bit. Are you going to hang up?'

'No, no. You're well worth it, darling. But if I get cut off, you'll know why. Might have to go and find some credit, behind my *ear*. But what are you *doing* there?'

'Oh, you know.'

'I see. I trust you, darling. Although I *may* have to come over there, then, *quite soon*, and see you, and . . . kiss you on the lips. Bit of kissing, bit of the old, er . . . bumming.'

'What? *Ewan*. Dear me.'

'Sorry. Letting the old mouth run away with me there. Can you imagine if you were here now, though?'

'Not really.'

I looked around the shadows of my borrowed accommodation. His voice was such a queer anachronism: so animated, where the room was still, and empty. And I was still.

'Well, *I* think we'd have a great laugh, to be honest,' he was saying. 'Get out of our tiny minds, I suspect . . .'

'Are you drunk now?'

'I've had a few bevs. I'm not drinking now, like. I'm in bed!'

'Okay. I was only asking.'

'Well – I know.'

'But how are you getting on down there, anyway? Do you like it yet?'

'Oh, well I do okay, you know me. I mean, I did feel like I was turning into a bit of a caricature of myself, to be honest, sometimes, before. Like the colours were drawn on too brightly, or the lines were too thick? . . . Hello? You still there?'

'I'm still here.'

'Good. Well, stay there. Stay on the line! So, yeah. Just a total fish out of water, to be honest. I'm like a lost sheep, and I need a guide *dog*. Ha!'

Ewan used to work in the HMV on Market Street, back in Manchester. I always thought he looked quite demonic behind his till there, with his pursed lips, and his ruddy face, and his cloud of fried, dark blond hair. He was apt to wrinkle up that bumpy nose and dart his lively eyes about, too, when demonstrating – for instance – how mental he was feeling. Or he might scratch his bristly chin, before pointing at me, and saying, 'You're mental, you.'

Yes, that was the sum of it, wasn't it?

'You *are* though,' he'd say, guiding me towards the bar, one hand on the small of my back. 'You're from the nutty regions. Most mental girl I *know* . . .'

Now I cast about for something else to ask him.

'Who are you living with, then?' I said. 'Are you on your own at last?'

'Oh no, I'm just with these . . . great lads,' he said, 'great bunch of lads, from the shop. I mean, they *are* great, like I say. They do make me laugh loads. I'm laughing my head off all day long, to be honest, but you know the type: fourteen haircuts between them, jeans like Everton mints, can't exactly take them seriously at all. But never mind about them. I don't care about them. Are *you* all right? You sound *happy*. Doing good, yeah? Smiles Davis? What are you *doing* over there? Tell me. What the effing jeff are you doing?'

'Hm . . . I don't know, Ewan. Maybe I'm just having a rest.'

'You're – hello? What was that?' he said.

'You're – hello? What was that?' I said.

'You're – Oh, my dear darling. Hello? You still there?'

'Yeah, sorry, I think it cut out then. Or I might have yawned.'

'You need a little napette. I'm quite tired myself, like, but, er, been meaning to *say* . . . do you know what would improve the quality of my life immeasurably right now?'

'I don't know.'

'A picture of your boobs . . .'

'Ah—'

'Would improve . . . quality . . . No, it would, though. Wouldn't it?'

'I don't think so.'

'*Im*-measurably . . .'

'*No* . . .'

'Wouldn't it?'

'Ewan, come on.'

'Well – okay. But, like I say, I just do miss you loads. So so much. Am I pushing my luck here?'

'It's not that. I mean, can't you just look at some generic boobs?'

'No.'

'No?'

'Hey, where'm I going to get some generic boobs at this time?'

'Let me rack my brains. The internet?'

'Don't fancy that, darling. No . . . Anyway, I want to see *your* boobs.'

'You want to see *some* boobs.'

'Don't say it like that. You're so down on yourself, you.'

'I'm really not. But – y'know, you've called me because my name begins with an A, haven't you?'

'What? Is that what you think? You're so wrong. So down on yourself. *Always* putting yourself down. You want to stop that, you know.'

'Christ, Ewan. Okay. Listen, give me a second.'

I sat up again then, pulled down the sheet and held up my phone and took a picture of my bare knees.

'Brace yourself,' I said.

'Hey, hold on. Incoming! What the *hell*?'

'Squint, Ewan.'

'Oh, my dear darling. Oh wow. You've blown my mind now. You look *hot*.'

'You think so? I'm not really in it, am I?'

'You do, though. Hey, don't say that. You know what I mean. Very hot.'

'Well. I don't know about that.'

'Hey, are you dead embarrassed now?'

'I'm mortified. I feel sick, and lost.'

'Well, *I* think you're a great girl.'

'Thanks. Well, just do me a favour and don't make that your screensaver or anything.'

'No, no, no. You're a *life* saver. I will use it wisely.'

'You don't have to do that.'

'I will use it. Thank you, darling. Ah darling, sorry, I am dead drunk, you know.'

'Mm . . . I thought as much.'

My own glass of water was on the floor, and I picked it up and tipped it back. It was awkwardly done, now I was lying down again. I coughed, and gripped the glass lightly in my teeth. Ewan's teeth were clamping together, too. I could hear them tapping, and his tongue clicking. Then he was making a whinnying sound. Then I think he knocked something over.

'. . . rrregional regions!' he was saying. 'They can't stop us! Hmmm . . . Grrr . . . Hello? You still there?'

'Just about.'

'Okay. Well, now I think you should *hold* your boobs.'

'No, I don't think so.'

'Language, darling. Hey, I don't mean for a photo, I just mean, if you like, just put the phone, like, *hold* the phone in place with your shoulder, then you can *hold* your boobs and keep talking to me.'

'No thanks.'

'Okay. Pushing my luck there. You're dead right. I must admit, though, I do think it's dead funny that you're like, dead clever, and you've just sent me a picture of your boobs.'

'It is funny,' I said.

'I'm not judging you.'

'Judge away.'

'Ah darling, you do no harm. And you know what else? No, listen, you'll like this. When I was rolling around in bed just then, a pound coin got stuck to my bare bum! If that's not a win-win situation then I don't know what is. I've embarrassed *no one* but myself. Oh, I wish *you* were here, though. We could kiss and . . . Hello? Hello? . . . Hello?'

3

'*Hello* . . .'

I whispered it, kneeling and rubbing my fingers together. My other hand was shielding my eyes. The sun was like a bright coin.

I hadn't seen this cat around before, though. Black and white, and heavy, currently she was rolling about underneath the basketball hoop in my building's back yard. Her prize, held in outstretched paws and yawned at – a baby's dummy.

Again I said, '*Hello* . . . *Hello there, Missy* . . . *Miss Puss.*'

This time I rubbed at the cotton of my dress: *swick, swick, swick.* At which she flipped slowly over onto her back, stretched out her bearded, pure white neck and yawned at me, too.

4

The streets were straight, endless, silent. The days pale and brilliant.

In the frame houses on College Avenue the curtains and blinds were kept drawn against the glare, and most of the gardens looked finally dishevelled. Maybe once per block there was the brisk ticking of a sprinkler and a tricked-out crop of dewy green, otherwise the lawns looked like the verges: like spills of old pouch tobacco. On Yew Street the weathered shingle houses put me in mind of paper wasps' nests, and the old cars in their drives looked no less blown. Were they really being lived in, these places? One pebbled plot stood out here: its cacti jamboree. Those thick, thorned tongues proclaimed a kind of rude health.

I walked this same route to Broad Ripple Village every morning, had my first cup of coffee there, sitting in the window of The Monon Café, looking out at the empty street. This 'village' was a very brief drag: one crossroads and a dozen businesses, each bearing a picture window and a cloth canopy, these casting their shadows on a chalk-white pavement.

Back at the apartment there was my notebook and my laptop, along with my reading glasses, plucking the sunlight across my hoary old cabbage of a thesaurus. On the bedroom floor was my water, my phone, my hand cream.

5

Two summers ago, idling by the gates of Gaskell House, astride her bike, next to my bike, like she was meeting me after school, Cathy used to say, 'How'd it go?'

Or, 'What d'you talk about?'

'Did you talk about me?' she'd say.

And, 'Does she hate your dad too now?'

('Who hates him?' I said.)

It was a horrible habit. I told her to stop, but then she just started seeing a priest on those days instead: Father Frank at the Holy Name, suddenly he was lending her books. Meeting me further down Oxford Road, she showed me these grisly volumes. *The Evidential Power of Beauty*, I remember her toting (just like she used to tote real books, in fact, yes in exactly that same way), and *Interior Freedom* and *More than a Carpenter*. She kept them in her bike basket.

'They're terrible books!' she said. And she said, '*He* says I'm unconvertible.'

And, 'I *am* pro-choice, it's not about that, Aislinn.'

I tried to palm her off on my friend Karl at around this time.

'Can you not take her away?' I said.

He wasn't having it, though.

'I do fancy Cathy,' he said. 'She's fit and everything. But I also know for a *fact*, that if I got involved with her I'd never achieve anything I wanted to in life.'

Which was quite something, when you thought about it.

I was on something of an efficiency drive myself back then, with regards to the people I knew. Not Cathy yet. I could cope with Cathy (I thought); but other people. Beginning, I think, with a very unpleasant day I'd spent with a man called Gareth, who'd recently moved down to London. I was happy he'd gone, so I couldn't tell you why I agreed to go down and visit him. For the train trip, maybe? But after we met up we had an aimless and soggy time. A wretched time, really.

'What do *you* want to do?' he kept saying. 'You've lived here before.'

So we ambled dumbly around a few bookshops, and after that we went drinking (well, he was drinking, I was on lime and soda), going from pub to pub in Soho, with everywhere we tried somehow an awful ill-fit, either too busy and convivial – which was shaming, with us the way we were, I had nothing to say to him, nothing at all, and he seemed to be getting increasingly desperate about that – or else too empty. We trod wet footprints into those establishments and then I'd look at us in the poxed bar-back mirrors, between bent postcards, clippings, injunctions: his hot, heavy drunken face and then my sober face, which was – a blank.

'I don't know where to go,' he kept saying. 'I don't know *anybody*. It's *impossible* to meet people here. Do you want another one of them?'

He was renting a room out in Zone 3. By the time our train slowed down for his station – which was deserted, and it can't have been later than ten o'clock – he'd started reminiscing about Manchester.

'I *dream* of moving back,' he said. 'I've never felt at home anywhere else.'

'Oh stop,' I said. And then, 'You're romanticising it. You're lucky you got out. You have a chance down here.'

He only sniffed at that, though, as he stood up. He'd always been comically tall. His new grey raincoat clinched him like a moth's tight wings.

'Don't you think it's romanticising it more to *stay there*?' he said.

And then the doors opened. I didn't stand up.

I'd met Gareth when I was twenty-three, after I'd done a reading at Bretton Hall in Leeds. He was a third-year English student there, and before I caught my train home, I sat opposite him in the empty canteen while he 'interviewed' me. He was wearing a tweed jacket and – cowboy boots, as I remember it. The tape in his Dictaphone had stopped turning after the second question but I didn't tell him. It sat on the greasy chrome table along with an old piss-yellow-paged copy of *Lucky Jim* that he'd brought me, thinking I'd like it. (I didn't like it.) When he finished his degree he moved to Manchester, got in touch, and spent the years that followed making various ill-starred attempts to get off with my female friends. One summer he invited Cathy and me to stay for a weekend at his parents' house in Cumbria. What I remember of those mornings is his mother fussing over us all in the kitchen, and how that made him huff. He'd stand in the doorway and huff, and then go out to have a cigarette in the garden. As we ate our breakfast we could see him sitting out there on a wrought-iron chair under an apple tree, the smoke masking his face.

In cutting people out, a phrase I found useful was: 'This is non-negotiable.' I enjoyed deploying that: it was effective; it made me feel peaceful. Something else I found myself saying was, 'I can't help you.' I'd have to keep saying that, to certain people, but again, it worked.

So who else had I let go?

There was Bronagh. She was probably the saddest of the lot; she used somehow to seep into my vicinity, when I was feeling low (quite a common kind of urban spectre, that, I think). When I moved into my new place in town she appeared and looked it all over. In my kitchen she pulled the shiny top off one of the taps.

'Yeah, it's just shit, really, isn't it?' she said, holding up the little silver cross. 'I mean, they finish these places to the lowest possible . . . And how much are you paying? Yeah, they're taking the piss, really.'

She put the piece down on the surface then and put her hands back into the pockets of her jeans. She stood there with her elbows out. Her dyed-black, chin-length hair, was, as always, brushed out into a fusty, static-y triangle.

I was already in my armchair and soon she installed herself opposite me, on the small, blockish settee. The assumed common ground on evenings like that was only ever baffled emotional hardship. To deviation from that point, Bronagh was not receptive, she was more or less – inanimate. There was only that constant coercion of me into her rueful 'we', her adenoidal, 'people like us, yeah?', this pursued with such dull doggedness, it was almost endearing. Almost. Some other people mightn't have found it so. I remember her telling me about a last-minute date she'd been on with a much older man who'd been coming more and more frequently into the bookshop where she worked.

'You know, it was funny,' she said, 'I just went straight out when he called, just still in my *brown* cardigan, hadn't shaved my legs, *no* make-up. It made me laugh. People were looking at us in the restaurant, and I thought, Yeah, well done, you're all living in a fucking dream world. How long is it since they were on the breadline? I'd been scrubbing my kitchen floor all afternoon, on my fucking hands and knees. I mean, is that okay with them?'

He didn't ask her out again. She kept emailing him, though.

'I just want to rub his face in it a bit,' she said. 'I'm funny like that, you know? He's living in a dream world; I'm struggling for survival. Supposed to be my friend, this guy. He could get me out of this hole with what he spent on his fucking overcoat, you know? Feel like pointing that out to him, actually. You know, don't come into the shop to look at me, like I'm some exotic bitch in a cage, don't ask me out and I'm supposed to listen to your life story, and your fucking dead wife and so on, and then, what, I'm not good enough to communicate with?

'I can't take it much longer, to be honest, you know, in that place,' she said. 'The customers are just too fucking stupid. I mean, I just walk off half of the time, when they're talking to me. And now they've put this old bitch on the desk with me, as well. Y'know, it's not enough they've already neutered you with their stupid shirts and name badges. Not a moment to myself, now. I mean, I'm thirty-six, man, I've heard it all. I really have. So shut the fuck up. I mean, please. I just refuse to talk, you know? I just refuse. And believe me, no amount of words could be worse than my silence. A dog knows when you don't want to deal with it, right? A dog knows. She doesn't know. You should come in and see her, actually. You'll recognise her. She looks like an old *boot*.'

There was another expedition, later that year, to London this time, to see a different man (she really was intrepid, that touched me sometimes).

'I mean, I go all that fucking way, and – nothing. He went out with his friends and left me in his flat. What happens to manners, you know? What is it with this apocalypse of manners in this country? He knew why I was there. He *knows*. I'm looking for a reason to stick around. I don't need another fucking *friend*. Do people think I'm stupid? That I need another fucking man emailing me his what-I've-done-today shit, you know? I mean, why?'

He was only twenty-two, that one. He used to work at the shop with her. They hadn't even kissed.

'It's not ab*out* that,' Bronagh said (she looked at me with infinite pity then). 'And age doesn't mean anything. *You* know. He should just grow the fuck up if he's thinking about my age. He's the one. He's the one who was, you know, sent me that postcard, and texting me at Christmas. I mean – why? I'd taken him a book down, you know, this CD I'd burned, because he said he was interested, then I just end up bringing them back with me again. I just put them in a bin on the train. And I tore that postcard he sent me up and left it on his desk, so, you know, he hopefully will get the fucking message now. Guy thinks he's a radical, well, no, take off those brightly coloured clothes and put the fucking suit on, you know? I mean, I like anal sex, I've done it a lot, no problem, am I supposed to lie about that?'

At last she met an unhappy man who worked in her shop's stockroom. His name was Wade. Again, a 'curtain's up' silence settled in my front room as she told how he'd left suddenly, and now she'd heard he'd died, after a short stay at a rehab clinic in south Wales.

'I think I knew, actually, yeah, I knew, that he was going to be dead soon,' she said.

'Never met anyone so broken, to be honest. Never have. You know when a CD case rattles – when you shake it? He was like that. Talking to him. That sound. Thirty-four, man. I mean they say it was alcohol caused it but, okay, physically, maybe, but it was all the abuse, you know. Fucking – Catholic Church. Guy had no chance. And we were very similar, you know, we really were.'

A while later, still very wistful, and on to her own mooted suicide now, she said, 'Well, when I do it, it *will* be final, you know, so . . . There'll be no risk of it not working. And I'm going to leave such a sarcastic note behind. I mean, *really* . . .'

I watched her walking around my flat, to the kitchen, to the bathroom – she had a funny walk; a weightless, puppet-like amble, very pitiful to see. She walked like that around the Arts room in the shop, too. I soon stopped going in there altogether, and I wasn't the only one.

'Could do without seeing her face, thanks,' Karl said. 'Encountering her *ire*. Is that in her job description, do you think, sourly judging people? Stuff's cheaper on the internet anyway. And let's face it, it's always nice to get a fucking parcel.'

You couldn't fault his logic.

And so, forgoing the bookshop, we walked towards the bus stop, him hunched up in the balding upholstery of his corduroy car coat, me grimacing against the bitter wind, my head wrapped Bedouin-style in a tartan scarf. This was in February last year.

'So, I came into town today to meet you for your birthday,' Karl said, 'but also because, well – just look at it.'

I shook my head. It felt like there were long fingers being pushed into my ears.

★

Up on the seventh floor of Whitworth House, Karl's rooms were cramping living quarters: one long room and a bathroom; all in the customary disarray that night. His grimy, glazed-tile coffee table showcased bowls and boxes ridged with weeks-old noodles, while full ashtrays and improvised ashtrays were docked on every surface: on the window sill, on the floor, along with apple cores in various stages of their withering. And then there were the books: un-shelved, and stacked all around the walls like dry-stone slates. I moved some papers from the sofa and sat down there, only to sink unpleasantly, slowly, as if into cold clay. It was a dreadful sensation. I stood up again smartly, and found two nearby hardbacks to use for a deck. *The World Is What It Is*, I think, and *A Temple of Texts*. I sat back down on them.

Meanwhile, Karl was over in the kitchen nook, stooped in deep conference, in solemn communion, with a cigarette and the hob's front plate. I watched him rolling the cigarette tip back and forth there, on the jelly-red glow. (I was glad. The smell of smoke could only be an improvement. The room's current smell I might have called '*Homme Seul*'.)

Still, mitigating the penned-in feel a little was

the picture window, which took up half of the front wall. Karl had his writing desk there – he was a playwright – although I don't know that the view detained him overmuch. On the evening I'm thinking about I remember him looking out and yawning.

He yawned and then started scratching at the back of his neck, where his dark, curly hair grew over the collar of his capacious denim shirt.

'Fuck's sake,' he said, and then he stretched both of his arms out in front of him and cricked his neck.

The air around this figure was marked with pale smudges of smoke, while before him, in the deep night, the falling snow now moved in shoals, and in places even seemed to be falling slowly upwards . . .

Out there was an empty car park and the railway bridge, its bricks the colour of burnt and greasy blood sausage. The old bank opposite hosted chipped and lumpy chimeras, these clustered under the ledges like old chewing gum. There were apartments in there now. I'd ended up at a party in one of those places one Christmas, and remembered now how looking for my coat I'd opened the wrong door; very much the wrong door, to a cold, messy bedroom, and an

Ikea lamp arcing over a crowded bed. I think there were five of them at it, and yes, all lowing like cattle.

'"I'm in hell,"' I said; 'that's her latest thing.'

'Hm?'

Karl turned around and squinted at me. With his arms folded, his long cigarette bobbed signals as he sucked on it.

'Bronagh,' I said. 'She says that to me, "I'm in hell," and then she just stands there. I don't disbelieve her, as it goes, but why tell me? It's poor form, isn't it?'

Karl took his cigarette out then, and scratched his forehead with his thumb.

'Yeah,' he said.

His eyes looked sore, too. I mean, as far as I could see. The only light came from that one small bulb in the cooker hood. His hair was receding, making his face look long and mournful. He had thin lips and sunken cheeks. He kept the cigarette gripped in his teeth, pointing upwards, as he leaned down and pulled off his boots, before taking a bowl from the table, tapping a shower of ash into it, and then sitting down opposite me. He held the bowl in his lap.

'Maybe,' he said at last, 'we should just chase her out of town and throw her off a cliff.'

'Yes,' I said, 'it's strange you should say that. I've had that thought before. Can you imagine? Her feeble little body falls and breaks . . . that ghastly look leaves her eyes for ever . . . and then, spring could start. Bluebirds and snowdrops. Maybe we could all come to life.'

'Yeah,' Karl said. Then, 'So do you want to go out again tonight?'

'No. It's too damn cold, isn't it?'

'You don't fancy just popping over to the Temple?'

I tipped back my head.

'*No*,' I said, and then, 'Do you not fancy stabbing yourself, in the temple, with a fork?'

He shrugged.

'I knew you were going to say that,' he said.

It was a bar he was talking about, one just behind his building, and a haunt of so many of those ursine, lately young men of Manchester. I made the mistake of going in there on my own once a few years back, looking for somewhere to contemplate some good news I'd had: a terrible failure of the imagination on my part (but then, that city encouraged them). I was minding my own business down there, standing waiting for my drink, when suddenly an arm was slung heavily around me, and I was having my shoulder squeezed by someone I barely knew, someone stubbly, and sticky.

'We're all dead proud of you, you know,' this sweaty person said, while his gathered friends smiled uneasily. In fact – yes, that's what that bar smelled of that night: rotten teeth.

I shrugged off the arm. It took two shrugs.

'Yeah . . .' he said, grinning. 'We are. No, we all are . . .'

But that was their thing, those denizens. I knew that. They were always shaking each other's hands and slapping each other's backs. I'd witnessed that before, witnessed it and always half-expected each back-slap recipient to cough up a little cloud of coffin dust; for a dry little feast of dust to spill down their chin . . .

Karl didn't mind it in there, but then he'd been on a drunk for a long time too, then. The pustules around his nose were ripening again, hotly conurbating with those on his forehead. The rash resembled watermelon flesh. Red wine fanged down his chin, that night in his flat; foaming pink up the bottle's neck each time he placed it back between his stockinged feet.

I was having a break from all that myself, I should say. I just had the can of Diet Coke I'd brought up with me. It had been in my coat pocket all afternoon and was still nicely chilled for that. I swilled it round my teeth, felt its dry fizz on my gums before swallowing.

'So are you going to see the lovely *Jim* while you're away?' Karl said.

'Oh,' I said, 'no. I don't think so. Damn it, what d'you have to bring him up for?'

'Yeah, sorry.'

He was lighting a new cigarette off the old one now, peering down at the operation with one eye pinched closed.

'Well, it's okay,' I said. 'It's a legitimate question, I suppose.'

It was, too. Jim was — someone I'd met in America, the first time I went there. He lived in New York; or he had done, anyway. But the thing was, as I found myself telling Karl, 'I don't know how I painted it to you at the time, but that argument we had was pretty final.'

'You said it was bad.'

'Bad hardly covers it.'

'Shit.'

'Argument probably doesn't cover it,' I said.

'Shit,' Karl said again. Then, 'How d'you mean?'

'Well, what was I arguing with, after all? He didn't seem like a very substantial phenomenon, when it came to it, who I was shouting at and pushing. And neither did I any more. I don't know if he'd become a ghost, or if I was some kind of savage ghost . . . I was so frightened, I think I became pure *id*.'

Karl had raised his eyebrows. I went on: 'I've never felt that before. That feeling of being trans-figured. I've even thought of going back there, back to Birmingham, just to see if there isn't some sign there: a crater in the pavement, maybe, or a rent in time . . . I don't know. If so, maybe I could . . . I don't know . . .'

'Fucking hell, Aislinn,' Karl said.

'Well—'

'But also, you know, I'm bound to say, if you will get involved with Americans . . .'

'Yes. No, you're right. They're queer fish. And pedantic. I was always saying things he didn't get. Things that seemed reasonable to me.'

'Did you – deny the moon landing?'

'Oh,' I said, 'no. Not me. Perhaps I should have done.'

Karl swigged his drink then. And I swigged some of mine, too. We sat there for a few moments like that, before he exhaled, performed a croak of a hiccup, and then wiped the back of his hand across his stained mouth.

'And you've not been in touch since?' he said.

'No. I mean, I sent him this stupid apology email that I hope never to have to think about again – and damn it, I just did – but, he didn't reply to that. So . . .'

'I think I'm going to cry,' Karl said.

'Oh, stop it. You brought him up.'

I tried to lean back on that awful settee of his then, but toppled, and had to sit back up, re-arrange the books under myself.

'Well, I think,' Karl was saying, 'that sometimes drunkenness and fatigue can lead to two people adopting positions which can become – opposed positions.'

'Well – *yes*,' I said. 'There is that.'

And then, because I couldn't help myself, and because Jim had been on my mind again recently, I went on, 'I mean, that's exactly what happened, of course, but it doesn't help me to know that. I just have this fuzzy, charged-up memory of myself shouting out all about what a fucking stupid motherfucker he was. And then he said I was "too literary". That was *his* new thing.'

'He said that?'

'Mm . . . He said all sorts, though. He was just making things up, I think. I felt for him on that account, in a way. He said, "I have to say I prefer you when you're *sober*. You were being so sweet earlier." Well – that was pulled out of the air, wasn't it? And then he said, "You would've gotten tired of me *so quickly*." Also – not true. But yes, "You're too literary." Stupid coincidence: *as* he first said it, looking at him, knowing what he was doing, that he had to not like me now, not even *like* me, I was thinking, I feel like the Panther, here, I feel like Josef K . . . And then, there it was: "You're too literary." He kept saying it, too, like he knew he'd found the right spot at last, the magic button . . . Which of course he *had*. And he couldn't even pronounce it: "too litter-y", he kept saying, "too litter-y, too dramatic", and then, "I am *not* litter-y." You know, in case I hadn't worked that out.'

'What a fuck nut,' Karl said. 'My God. Why didn't he just shit in your head?'

'Well yes, quite. That took everything away from me. Very effectively. The way he was looking at me, too. Like he couldn't wait to start walking away. I even suspect he's still doing that, some- times, which is – a funny feeling, sometimes.'

'Yeah,' Karl said.

I went on, 'And I couldn't work after that, which made everything worse. Self-pity, you know – makes your voice thick. Terrifying situ- ation. Damn it, I'm angry now. I do believe life is loss, I do, but my suffering-to-words ratio was out of control: lying around composing nothing but these – righteous arias, month after month, these tawdry special pleas. Such rich concoctions, really. And then there was what I washed them down with . . .'

Karl had tipped his head back at some point during that speech, though, and now I watched him slowly blow out a shuddering spume of smoke. It rippled towards the low ceiling, ravelling white like spaghetti.

'So,' he said at last, 'that was last year.'

'Mm . . . That went on for two years.'

'Shit, Aislinn.'

'Yes,' I said, 'it was difficult. But necessary, I think. Or unavoidable, at least. He was doing what he had to do. As was I: being in the middle of a comprehensive nervous breakdown. So – there you go. What else could have happened? Wires get tripped in a life, don't they? Our wires were already tripped. And we're all only at the mercy of those . . . impetuses, I'm afraid, for however long they last.'

'Yeah,' Karl said, 'for however many fucking, shit years.'

'Mm . . .' I said. 'Well, you are, though. I think you're lucky if they don't last your whole life, frankly. So – will I see him again? I don't know. I'd like to, before the end, but maybe that's pedantic of me. Sometimes I feel like we are together, in a way. In a very *distant* way . . . He's part of my cosmos, maybe, is a way to put it. Sometimes I feel like that. At other times it's more like this – deficit, inside. I don't know if either of those feelings is the right one.'

'No,' Karl said.

'But it was shame I felt afterwards, most of all.'

'Mm . . .' He was narrowing his eyes at me now. '*Shame was warehousing in his liver,*' he said.

'Who's that?'

'That's – Norman Mailer, I think.'

'Well, I know that feeling, but it was not hepatic in this instance. Or – not entirely. I don't know why it took hold of me the way that it did. Well, I do know, it's because I was vile. Like, Leontes-vile. So, there was that. Also, I've never really *had* an argument before. Barring those spats with my mum. It's not something I do. Who am I going to argue with? And yet suddenly this poisonous new seam opened up, and then – the shame of it. I came round the next day, painfully, and it was in me. And un-metabolisable, too, for a long time.'

'Mm . . .' Karl said. 'Shame doesn't go away, does it?'

I shook my head.

'I don't know. I'm going to say that it doesn't go away if you don't make the effort to shift it. I think it degrades very slowly. But like anything, to tolerate it is to venerate it in the end, isn't it? I mean – don't you think? I'd call shame a cuckoo. There's something lewd, triumphalist about it, once it's in you. The way it edges you out of yourself. I was ashamed, and then I was ashamed of my shame. All these discordant fields of stress . . .'

'Yeah,' Karl said again.

So – Karl was a good friend, but the person I'd always considered my best friend was a man I rarely saw. Erwin was living in Newcastle when we met (I was in London then), and later he moved to France, where he still is, as far as I know. He's a poet, and we first came upon each other in 1996, on one of my only nights out in London, at a reading in the deep, dark and beer-y back room of a pub in Clerkenwell. He was the last to read – on a stage hung with copies of the pamphlet that was being launched, these suspended on lengths of fishing line – and after that (he was very good, I thought), we continued to talk out on the pavement, where he'd gone to have a cigarette. He looked cold as he stood out there. He looked stiff and suspicious, until he laughed – I made him laugh – and then he bent forward, tilting from where his arms were folded. He was my age and my height. He had sunken grey eyes, and coarse, curly red hair, already thinning on top.

After that first night, when we got along so well, there were a couple of proposed further meetings that finally one or both of us couldn't make. Nearly a year passed before we again came face to face, on a bright and rainy October afternoon, again in London. He greeted me then by tilting his chin up and narrowing his eyes. He'd saved me a seat with the Tesco bag he carried his things in. The same bag he'd had in Clerkenwell? Yes, it looked like it could have been. The third and last time we met – before we both moved away, we were both twenty-one – was at the height of summer, and to that rendezvous he wore shorts. It was then I realised that this was a man possessed of a confidence that bordered on slyness. That could have over-whelmed me; instead, I decided to match his slyness with my own. I liked his emails, when he started to send them, very much. They seemed courtly, too, in a way. The second time he wrote, he finished with:

> In the spirit of sincerity, and hopefully to amuse you, I've attached a poem. But – only read it if you want to.

Mostly we talked about books we'd read and were reading. (Occasionally, too, he recounted dreams he'd had that had featured me.) Sometimes we read the same book at the same time and discussed it. Other matters were – not addressed directly. Once he wrote, *I'm suffering with a terrible cold.*

I'm sorry you're ill, Erwin, I said. *I hope you feel better soon. Please take care of yourself.* And last year I told him, *My new flat's depressing me.*

He replied with, *I'm sorry to hear your flat is depressing you. Try to take a walk every morning if you can, Aislinn – I know the weather is dreadful.*

Nine years we kept that up for. A long time. Far too long, probably.

6

And now the weeks were passing in Broad Ripple.

Here I was – walking one early morning along the river path. The White River, that was, now bottle-glass brown, and progressing slowly through the park. I picked my way along deep banks hackled with dry reeds.

The swimming pool was an unlikely oxbow lake: empty at this hour, and holding quiet webs of sunlight in sway: like a vast block of jelly had been sunk there in the yard. I took off my sandals and sat down. The water was still night cold. It was cold like an icebox plum, and gripped me. I felt the stubble thistling on my shins, the goose-flesh creeping up the backs of my arms . . . I leaned back and tilted my face to the sun.

There were bonds that that plane journey had always so beautifully dissolved. That's what I was thinking about then; about my dodge and how it was restored; until here I was again: away. Peaceful again. Able to think.

To think about Jim, for instance. He'd grown up in a place like this, of course. Or – this was how I used to imagine it anyway.

It took me eight months to call the long number he'd given me the morning after we first met. I was living at Cathy's place by then.

That bit of paper I'd kept also held his home address (this illustrated with a stick man holding a large envelope), and his email address. (*For when you are playing on your computer!!* he'd written.) Still, sitting on my bed, listening first to that transatlantic chittering and then to that ringing that sounded off-key, I felt vertiginous, sick. I found I was leaning right forward. I hope it doesn't sound fatuous if I say it wasn't at all clear to me that he ever wanted me to get in touch.

When his machine clicked in I didn't leave a message. A few minutes later I tried again, again leaning forward, and that time I did speak. He didn't call back. It was another six months before I heard from him, and then he was in England, on tour, and was calling to say he was due in Manchester.

'*Um, tomorrow night, I guess?*'

★

It always happened like that. I mean – I think it happened a dozen times over the next three years, before his bookings dried up altogether. If he wasn't playing Manchester, I'd get the train to Liverpool, Leeds; wherever he was. On those mid-afternoon train journeys I used to sit with this – funny new poise, I remember.

I met his band-mates for the first time in Manchester: Maxey and Ezra. They'd played together since school, and were all the same age (twenty-seven then, I was twenty-two), but the other two looked older than Jim: both being big – American-big, their T-shirts draped them like dust-sheets – and Ezra was already balding, retaining just a monkish fringe of sandy blond hair. Jim was the youngest in his family, too, he told me, the youngest of eight in 'a, like, boringly typical Midwest, Catholic family'. I could have guessed that, though – the large family part, I mean – seeing how he was among other people that night. He let himself be babied when it suited: turning to Maxey or Ezra to answer questions that were directed at him, for instance (I kept noticing that), and then there was that helpless way he had – screwing up his face and balling his fists, rocking back on his stool and suddenly wincing, having drunk all of the drinks put down in front of him.

His smile was as sudden as a baby's. His teeth always looked very white to me: because he was so tanned, maybe? Or maybe because his thin lips turned puce when he drank. His tanned forearms, I remembered, and thought about, and how ghostly white the long fingernails of his right hand looked, too, gripping his glass, or the back of his neck. The night we met, he told me he had a thing about washing his hands.

'Ya, it's kind of an OCD,' he said.

And later, coming back from the restroom for the fourth time, wiping his hands on his jeans, he said: 'So I guess this is just *one* of my stupid compulsions that'll come to, like, *agitate* you, over time?'

(I knew what he was doing, but what had that made me think? Only of how Emma's nails had looked to Charles Bovary: 'cleaner than Dieppe ivory'. Yes, I really thought that.)

In Manchester, that first time, we finally sat down together in a mildewed corner of The Castle's saloon, next to the gutted piano, in the glow of the cigarette machine. He smiled at me then (those little white teeth) and I was smiling, too, really quite happy, and then he put down his glass, and gripped the edge of his seat, and said: 'So I should tell you that I'm actually *dating* someone right now?'

'Okay,' I said.

It was okay – what else could it be? – but he looked pained, and sympathetic, even biting his bottom lip now, and with his shoulders still braced in that apologetic sort of half-shrug. Yes, it was the way that he told me that irked me, that seemed so casually annihilating. Better get used to it, though, because subsequently when we met he always started off by telling me something like that, and always in that same sickly rueful way.

His speaking voice was funny: atonal and sing-song; so – bored-sounding and precious-sounding all at once. There was nothing attractive about it. But there was something compelling about it (I found). About its helpless sly piety. Now – who's this for? I used to wonder (because certainly it wasn't for me, it couldn't have been, could it?) when he would sit there and say this, for instance: 'I mean, it's been four months now, so I feel like I should at least see it through with this girl? At least, like, do her that courtesy?'

Or, 'We did split up a month ago, actually, but she was pretty adamant we get back together, so . . .'

Looking at me sideways if he looked at me at all, he always talked as though these situations were pitiably out of his control. And – they *were*, I quickly realised, him being him.

And me being me . . .

He could never comprehend why I didn't date people. He asked me about that again and again; every time we met.

'But you *never* date *anybody*?'

'No. Why would I?' I said. 'Like who?'

Or sometimes I said, 'What would be in that for me?' Or, 'Would you feel better if I did?'

'Well – I *have* to be dating somebody, I just – have to be,' he said.

'Really? Even the idea of it for me . . . No. It would be like being lowered into wet concrete, wouldn't it? Don't you think? Too lonely-making.'

It's hard to remember what else we talked about. We talked occasionally about the writing we did. I remember telling him once about the terrible aversion I could develop to the practice.

'I have to get to the point where my only two options are: to do the writing or to kill myself,' I said. 'My aversion is commensurate to my will, so it's tough. Every word gets to be like a steamer trunk. I hate it.'

'Oh,' he said, 'huh. Well, I guess it doesn't come down to that for me . . . I mean, I do have some, like, moralistic dilemmas, I guess, just because what I write can be pretty *mean* about people, sometimes.'

'Really? Hm . . . That's just something to say, isn't it? No, I never quite believe people when they say things like that. Your songs aren't mean, Jim. Jesus. Other people are mean. As in: lacking. Also – the ones who whinge to you about mean-ness, I guarantee you, deep in their souls they're the ones who long for it. Don't pander to them. They'll only eat it up and then where are you?'

He didn't say anything to that, though.

His reading seemed limited, but he did read, so we could talk about books up to a point. We drank a lot. Meanwhile what he seemed keenest to discuss were, as I say, his girlfriends, also his ex-girlfriends, his ex-fiancée, his ex-wife. In each case it seemed to have taken about six months for him first to notice and then in short order begin to resent, very deeply, certain deficiencies in these women: in their ambitions, or in their care of him. Something else I noticed during these conversations: he was keen to co-opt any protest they might register.

As in: 'Mindy actually ended up throwing a drink in my face, but I, like, really respected her for doing that, actually.'

Or: 'Jo-Jo actually stopped answering the phone to me, but I, like, had a lot of respect for her, actually, for calling time like that.'

He would keep telling me how much he respected these women. I mean, in fact I got the impression that he felt less than nothing for them, and drew them all the closer for that. This closeness assuaging – what, exactly? That I couldn't tell.

'Listen, stop annexing what other people do,' I told him. 'It's their pissy gesture, not yours.'

'Oh,' he said, 'I hadn't thought of it like that. Ya, I guess that is pretty obnoxious, right?'

'Do you respect me so much, actually, for pointing it out?' I said.

'Huh?'

I was never sure when he was trying to provoke me. The things he said were so – naked, sometimes. Once he'd told me: 'My mom has gotten down *on her knees*, literally *on her knees*, apologising to me for my childhood. For not ever being there. But – that's no good to me now, is it?'

'No . . .' I said. 'Next question.'

And more than once he'd asked: 'What we felt when we met, that – *transcendence* – do you think that was just because of the *time* we met? I mean, I was at an all-time low that summer.'

That one I couldn't answer.

'I'd call that a moot point,' I said.

What else? How about this. He told me: 'You know when my mom listened to this new record she said, "Oh, poor little Jimmy, still looking for someone to really love you."'

A pretty outrageous thing to say, I thought. Well – wasn't it? Or was this how people talked to each other over there? I never knew how to react. I didn't react, in fact, is what happened.

We didn't sleep together again, after that first time. I suppose that might seem unusual. We'd share a bed, if not at my place, then splitting the cost of a hotel, but – we were always drunk: I remember above all walking drunk down long musty corridors with Jim – the vine-patterned carpets; the Anaglyptic wallpaper; the broken smoke alarms, their popped covers like aspirins set to sink and fizz – and him seeming so out of place there, so – 'unlikely' always: everything about him seemed unlikely. That long, checked overcoat of his, for instance, meant for far worse winters than ours. Iron-cold winters. I'd see that hung up sometimes, or slung on the back of a chair when he was out of the room, and it seemed like the eeriest artefact.

Beyond that – when it came to sex, I mean – the truth was I had no impulses in that direction back then. No impulses at all. It occurred to me later that maybe he didn't either. Not really. For whatever reason. He'd kiss me on the cheek and then lie back down again, look dully over at me. Sometimes he'd put one hand on my waist and then not move it, and keep looking at me. I liked to put my hand on his forehead, or over his eyes. We were like children, maybe. (Were we?) Two children fallen in love. Or – I don't know what to call it. Waking up with him there was so strange, I didn't ever dare put my arm around him, or – anything like that. I felt too afraid, overwhelmed.

I couldn't know what he was like with other people. Similar, I'd imagine: this seemed to be him. For myself, there hadn't been anybody else.

And then – the strangest thing: the last time I saw him (before our row), I didn't recognise him. I looked right at him (so he said) and then just kept walking, to the back of the Leeds University Students' Union still scanning all of those other faces: teenagers crowded round quiz machines, I was looking at.

Later Jim explained: 'Ya, I guess I decided not to cut my hair until my *life* is in better shape.'

Single for once, my impression was that he'd been saying this same thing to a lot of people back then though, and then looking out at them like that, like he was looking out at me then, through the crenels, as it were, above his new beard. (Well, you have to keep looking, don't you?)

Still – it wasn't long after that, after he'd gone home again, that I had a phone call from him saying he was going to fly *back* over, just to see me this time.

'I mean, we probably should just sort this out,' he said. And then he huffed.

And just a month later – at the end of November – I was at Piccadilly Station, on my way to the airport to meet him. It was seven a.m., and icy cold. My hands were frozen, and my breath came in slow silver clouds. I can't say any more what else I felt then or what I was thinking; if I ever really believed he'd come. I had tidied my flat. I hadn't been sleeping. That funny poise? No, that was gone, there was something else. Again – I can't say what it was any more. My phone rang while I was in the ticket queue.

'Ya, I wanted to catch you before you set off?' Jim said.

And then: he had a meeting, he said.

'And this is, like, life and death for me, so . . .'

'Okay,' I said.

The call lasted twenty seconds, no more. I'm not sure I spoke beyond saying, 'Okay.' I think I said, 'Well, no worries.' He hung up first.

I got an email from him the next day, and then, a few days later, a message to the same effect on my phone's voicemail: he was sorry for having to break our plans. I couldn't reply, in either case. It was a week before I called him back. He sounded bored though, by then. He was still talking about this meeting as if it had really happened, too, which was − strange, I thought. (Although − again, touching in a way, I suppose.)

'Well, maybe I could come over there,' I said.

'Oh,' he said. 'Um . . .'

So − what can you do? I wrote another book. In that book he was a playwright. It was difficult to write. I let everything else slide so I could do it. I lost my flat (that is to say, I shucked it off, more or less, I remember screaming at my mum to fuck off; all I could do was keep telling her to fuck off and go fuck herself when she kept asking what I was doing, what was I thinking, people work their *whole lives*, etc., etc.). I wasn't thinking. I used what money I had left to go to New York again the following summer. Although − as it turned out, that didn't work like it used to, being over there. Horrible to realise that, that my trick was broken, useless. I felt frightened and helpless.

I didn't see or hear from Jim again for two years, not until Birmingham, which was – strange to say – nearly three years ago now. What to say about that night? For a long time I couldn't even think about it.

It was summer – late August – but the band-room was cold, I remember, and dank, and pulsing with the din of the soundcheck upstairs. Greasy smudges ghosted the walls behind plastic chairs and a faded, black fabric sofa. The walls were woodchip, and graffitied floor to ceiling: here were spiky signatures, phone numbers, various pictographs. A low table held two bottles of Smirnoff, one of Jack Daniel's and half a dozen cans of Coke and Red Bull. Jim had come back before I'd decided where to sit.

'Oh, hey,' he said. 'You found it.'

He sat down on the sofa, and so I sat opposite, pulling up one of those chairs. He'd come back from the bar with an open bottle of red wine and two scuffed plastic wineglasses, set down on the table now.

'I'll pass on that, thanks,' I said, lifting up the vodka. 'Can I have some of this instead?'

'Oh. Ya, sure.'

In fact, it was worse than that: before I poured my drink (I used a plastic Dixie cup from the stack) I lay my wineglass on its side there between us, like a fallen chess piece or something. That seems particularly pathetic, looking back, and – cruel even (does it?), or – thuggish even. I don't think he noticed particularly, so that's something to be grateful for, but still. (Red wine has always made me ill, but he wasn't to know that, being as – and this was the source of my welling sadness and ire then – sharing bottles of wine wasn't something we did. Whatever he had it in mind for us to sanctify here, I couldn't do it.)

Pouring out his own drink, holding that scarred little camping glass steady, he said, 'So did you bring your new book along? So we can do our, like, traditional, formal swap.'

'I did,' I said, and I pulled my bag up onto my knees and took out the photocopy I'd had done that morning; in return he put his new record on the table, pushed it across to me.

'It's like, um, stories about different characters in a town, I guess,' he said, turning over the first pages of my manuscript, as I picked up his CD and turned that over, read the song titles.

'I see. *Winesburg, Ohio*.'

'Mm . . . What's that?'

'Stories in a town. You know, I think when we first met you were planning to write a record like this.'

'Oh, was I? Ha. Well, six years later. Ya, I think I just – did finally get bored of writing about myself, you know?'

If I'd have taken the wine, I remember thinking, this would have been the time to smile and say something rueful and sickly myself, wouldn't it? What nonsense. I couldn't do it. Instead I said: 'That's a shame. Really?'

'Well,' he said, shrugging. 'Okay. I don't know if it's that I'm bored, maybe just *tired*. Actually, this is something that I've been saying recently: that having given up on, or, like, rejected religion when I was in my teens, I think in this last year or two I have, like, finally, finally given up on romantic love . . .'

'Okay,' I said.

'. . . as something that exists, or that is going to save me, or – make life meaningful, at all. I think I just got so tired of believing that, and being disappointed. It's – all a lie,' he said, laughing, and then he rubbed one eye, and turned his mouth down at the corners for a second. 'So,

I just tried to write something more – external, I guess?'

'Okay,' I said again. And again I looked at the CD. 'Well – I'll look forward to listening.'

Jim winced. 'Well, anyways,' he said. 'So I had another birthday last week. Thirty-*three* now. We all had a, um, pizza party, up in Glasgow? And hired some go-karts? So – that was super fun.'

'Mm . . .' I said. 'Yes, I know it was your birthday. I got you something.'

I'd bought him a film that afternoon. Having got to Birmingham early, far too early, I'd had some vodka tonics and hit the Bullring.

'There you go,' I said, handing him the little HMV bag. 'Happy birthday to you. Happy half birthday to me.'

'Oh,' he said. 'That's sweet of you. Thank you.'

He said that, but he looked pained, if I'm honest. Taking the DVD out, reading the back, again he said, 'Oh,' and then, 'I nearly saw this last year, actually. I tried to, but I got to the theatre late, so . . . had to watch something else, which was – not so great.'

'Bummer,' I said. 'Well, this is really good. I saw it in New York last year, and it was so stunning, I went straight back in to watch it again. I've liked all of his films, though. I'm quite mad about him,' I said, reaching over and tapping the director's name:

Desplechin

'Oh, I don't know him,' Jim said. 'I just thought it looked interesting . . . So, wait – you were in New York last year?'

'I was. All summer. I was subletting.'

'So wait, you would have gone to see this in the Loewe's opposite Lincoln Center? That's where this was on, right?'

'Yes. Oh. You did, too? Not on the Friday?'

Now he was frowning.

'Wow,' I said. 'That's funny.'

And then I said, 'So – have you moved back? I thought you'd left, though?'

'Oh. No, I'm actually in Portland these days, but I was back there for the summer, subletting a friend's place too, actually.'

'Right. Okay.'

But he was still frowning.

'Huh. That is kind of funny. I don't know what I'd have done if I would have run into you there . . .'

'No . . .' I said. And here I leaned forward to get myself a refill.

'Do you want some?' I said.

But — no, he said, he was good. He poured himself another glass of wine, then turned some pages of my manuscript, which was still on the table. I watched him read half a page, at about a hundred pages in.

'You know,' he said, looking up, 'Ezra and Maxey always had, like, such a crush on you. They were always, like, so, so keen for me to get together with you. This English *author*.'

'Great,' I said.

'And now this woman that I've been dating . . .'

Here it came. I remember frowning down at my drink, checking myself and looking up again, back at him, who wasn't looking at me any more, as he hit his stride now.

'. . . she is, like, *so* worried about you. Because *she* wants to write. And she's, like, totally cool with all my other exes, and my ex-wife, it doesn't bother her at all, she is *so cool* with them, but she is, like, *so* worried about you.'

'Right,' I said. 'Okay. So what does she do now? She's a student, is she?'

'Oh. No. She's, um, a journalist? A lifestyle journalist; so that's like fashion, and gossip. Ya, she hates it. She, like, hates what she does *so* much, she knows it's ridiculous and worthless, but she wants to really write a book, and, um, be a real author, so . . .'

'I see. Why would you tell her about me then?'

'Oh. I don't know. I guess we were talking about writing?'

'Right,' I said. And then lifting my cup to him, I said, 'Okay. Good luck to her in her − real author-ing, then.'

'Well, we actually live together now,' Jim said. 'So . . . I mean, she moved out to Portland last year.'

'From?'

'Oh, from New York. I met her in New York, last year, so . . .'

'Right. Goodness. That's a long way.'

'Well, it was as much for her career as to be with me, so − I was happy for her to do that, you know. I mean, she was looking to move somewhere cheaper, cut her living expenses and so on, and we had been seeing each other over the summer, so I guess she was keen to pursue that, also . . .'

I'd emptied my cup and was pouring myself another drink when Ezra's bald head appeared through the curtain.

'We good?' he said to Jim. He raised a hand to me, too.

'Hey, Aislinn.'

'Hello, Ezra,' I said, and I raised my little red plastic beaker to him, now.

'Okay,' Jim said. 'Well – looks like I'd better get ready to do my thing.'

He stretched his arms out in front of him, and then rubbed his face.

'I'll see you later?' he said. 'You're sticking around?'

'Mm . . .' I said, standing up and taking my bag.

I took my drink upstairs, finished it, bought another, drank that in one . . . Jim was necking drinks on stage, too; whatever was passed up to him he tipped back his head and chugged, as the thirty or so people in the audience cheered and shouted and laughed to each other.

In front of me, one large, bowling-ball-calved man, in a black tour shirt and long, black shorts kept shouting, 'Jim-may!' and, 'Yeah!' He was filming everything on his phone, too. Between songs Jim was garrulous, and obscene. He lifted his plaid shirt up and rubbed the white hump of his belly; with his free hand he pointed up, and then pointed at himself, drilling his finger into his temple.

He said, 'We have so many friends in England and we always have such a super fun time here with you sexy-ass motherfuckers!'

'Jim-may! Yeah!' the fat man called out. He looked so excited, his eyes were wide and his face was running with sweat, dyed by the spot-lights, jelly red and cerulean blue.

'We should hang out more, Birming-ham!' Jim said.

Blackout. Another club. A revolving dance floor, I remember, and neon lightning bolts on the ceiling. There were holes punched in the walls and the pillars of the bar we were sitting at were padded like the posts of a wrestling ring, with this mealy, tooth-plaque-coloured foam. But I was drunk enough by then that I couldn't feel my hands any more, or the bottom half of my face. I was leaning heavily on the bar, looking at Jim, and tearing chunks off the foam, making a nice little pile of them in front of me.

'Have you never, like, wondered,' Jim was saying, 'why you and I never, like, made a go of it, with either me moving here or you moving out to me?'

'No,' I said.

I gave Jim a little boulder of foam then, placed it in his hand.

'Thank you,' he said.

'Made a go of what?' I said.

'Oh.' He shrugged. 'Okay.'

Taking his hand away he wiped his face. 'Well, I guess that's why then. I guess that's why,' he said.

For a while after that he just glowered there next to me, gripping his plastic glass and staring straight ahead. His face was flushed; his hair, cut short and neat now (as if that needs saying), was sweaty. I don't know that I'd ever liked him more than I did then, or felt happier to be sitting with him. When at last he turned back to me he seemed to react to my thinking that. He reacted like – I'd spilled something on him, standing up and stepping away from me, shaking his head and curling his lip. So there it was: the row. Suddenly we really were in it.

I don't remember leaving the club, but evidently – we left, through the back door, to take our marks out in the warm, wet night, among the tank-like bottle bins and the running gutters. I had my arms folded and Jim was the same: arms folded tightly.

'If you *felt* that way,' he was saying, 'why didn't you keep in touch with me more? *Huh?*'

And then he raised his eyebrows at me, looking at me, smirking at me, like I was stupid.

'*What?*' I said.

Or did I say that? Again – did I just think it? Because for all that I was very drunk, I could see what was happening now, with him. I could see quite clearly how all of that piety he claimed to have 'like, rejected' was rallying for him with terrific force then. Really – terrific force. No, I won't come back from this, I thought. And it was then that I took a deep breath and started shouting myself.

'*Who is this fucking woman?*' I said. '*Is she some kind of supermodel, is that it? What is this shit?*'

Jim smiled a very sickly, smug smile then, as he shook his head, and then he was shouting, too, cocking his chin up before he started.

'*No. Uh-uh.* She is a wreck, okay, she is a *wreck!*'

We were standing a few feet apart, and I couldn't seem to breathe quickly enough.

Well – something was rallying for me, too, now. Gall, could I call it? I could taste something like that, at the back of my mouth. The tarnish, pooling. I licked my teeth, tipped my head back for a second.

'Oh, perfect! Let me guess. Dead mother? Over-achieving sister? Used to be anorexic . . .'

'Okay, now you're being *callous!*'

'Yeah, yeah, everyone says that. Thing is, I'm

right though, aren't I? Of course I am. See, I'm gifted with that kind of intuition, Jim, which is why I'm an actual fucking writer as opposed to *a fantasist*. "Wants to write." *Jesus H. Christ*. You're like Kane building the opera house. She isn't going to finish a novel, I'll tell you that for nothing. So – those days when you're congratulating yourself on your life, 'cause you both have been "writing" all day: she hasn't. She's waiting for you to forget she said that.'

He held up his hands, looked away.

'Okay, I don't even know what you're *talking* about now!'

'Yes, you do. Oh, and how does she feel about your not-believing-in-love nonsense, incidentally? Let me guess, does she not believe in love either now? How cute. What a great couple!'

'She and I have a *difference of opinion*, okay! We have *a difference of opinion*!'

'Sorry, I'm just imagining this first date. She "wants to write". You really love John Fante. What a connection! I don't believe in love. Oh, no, "me either". What are you *doing*?'

But he was already shouting back: 'You know what I'm doing? I am *trying* to be polite to you, okay? *Okay?*'

'Are you?' I said. 'Is this polite? *She's so worried*

about you. My friends have a crush on you. She *"wants to write"*. Was I supposed to *blush*? Do you know what that is – "wants to write"? That's a cute thing that a moron says on a first date with you. You're not supposed to buy it, you know. You're not supposed to run with it. *I'm* a writer. *I* am. You're insulting me.'

'You know what? I would date a *janitor*, if it felt right!'

'Oh yeah, you'd love that, wouldn't you?'

'I cannot let you *disparage* my friend!'

'Who you don't love. No, sure. But you pair can take the piss out of me, right? This whole thing takes the piss out of me. "Wants to write". You're going to try to marry her for that, aren't you? No, you will, I can see it, it's your default, and here's how . . . No *listen*,' I said, because he was shaking his head again, and smiling in that ugly way again, 'the day you realise what a bust she is, that's the day you'll ask her, just to lance that boil and buy some time. No, you will. I don't *think* you'll go through with it, though . . . Christ, you people are so fucking easy to read. It's not even fun any more.'

'You know what? You and I don't actually *know* each other, so . . .'

'*What?*'

But he didn't say anything else then, he was just looking at me.

'This is such nonsense,' I said. 'You're saying you don't love me now? Be serious!'

'I *do* love you!'

'No, you *don't!*' I said, and I pushed him for the first time then, because I couldn't stand it any more. He stepped back, stumbled.

'I *dare* you to touch me again,' he said. 'I *dare* you to touch me *again!*'

So then – frightened, and – crying, I realised, and – with my throat tight, and feeling neither drunk nor sober now, I became discursive again. It was like I was in a discursive *swoon* suddenly.

'Well, yes, who would love this, I suppose, in this condition . . . ? It's a Catch 22, really, isn't it, not being loved, except I can't even say that to you because it's "literary" . . . "*That nothing cures.*" I can't say that. So what do I do?'

I was looking at him for help then. Nothing. He looked fidgety, deeply uneasy.

'Why didn't you show up?' I said. 'I was at the *station*. Had you even bought a ticket? There wasn't a meeting, was there?'

He looked furious now.

'Okay, listen!' he said. 'Listen! I bottled it, okay! I *bottled* it. It was not exactly a *lie!*'

'I don't care if it was a lie! It was your idea. You just cut me out. Is it how I look? What is it?'

But he was already shaking his head.

'You know what happened? It didn't feel right. Okay? *It – didn't – feel – right. Okay?* You know, I *have* and I *do* apologise to you for not calling to let you know sooner. That would have been courteous. I *have* and I *do* apologise for that!'

'*Courteous?* Oh my God. Oh my God . . .'

Well – that was the end. I don't think I even knew where I was after that. Some new inimical realm . . . That was all I knew. And on it went: Jim's face twisted up now, his nose creased to a snout, his white teeth bared as he went on shouting: he preferred me when I was *sober*, again: I was too literary, etc., etc.

'I am *not* your fucking playwright! *Okay?*' he said. '*Okay?*'

He was standing with his back straight and bawling at me, like he was shouting instructions to his team. Except that while he'd been going on this had occurred to me:

'Hey, is this a test?' I said. 'I used to think you were testing me, trying to make me say things . . .'

'No. *Uh-uh*. Maybe in the *past*, I did things like that, but *not now*. It is *too late* for that now!

Okay? I did *not* have to see you, you know. Kirsten did *not* want me to but I got in touch out of *courtesy* to you and . . .'

He had to tell me her name, didn't he? Well, I couldn't listen to any more of that, I couldn't continue. As I say, I was in my own realm now, quite far beyond all this 'courtesy' business and this 'Kirsten' business. What I said next did surprise me, because it was absolutely true, yet hadn't quite occurred to me before. Still, it's painful to remember, the tone of my voice saying it, and how he looked hearing it. He had his mouth turned down at the corners, his arms tightly folded, still. He'd started looking off to the end of the street, too, wanting very badly to get away.

'Jim, listen,' I said, 'please. I'm really bad at making my life better. Making real improvements. I've never known how to do it. I just think . . .'

He shook his head then, and again, looked away. I was very drunk. I closed my eyes to try to set myself straight, but when I opened them again he was already at the end of the alley somehow. I watched him raise his arm there, and then open a door . . .

And what I remember about that is – among all of the frightening feelings that I had then

– how, above all, I felt sorry to have done that
to him. Is that a strange thing to say? It seems
to me that it might be. But I remember that:
how seeing Jim like that, with his chin held up
like that, staring straight ahead as the cab moved
off, I felt – responsible, implicated, and terribly
sorry.

7

In Broad Ripple at three o'clock in the morning, there was only one place open on Prospect Avenue: in a row of shuttered fronts, looking like a rose-red lantern, Radio, Radio, spilling punk music into the soft emptiness of the street.

The man I sat down next to was drunk, and his drunken expression was: dazed incredulity. I watched him in the bar-back mirror while I waited to get served. He had his eyebrows raised, winched high to counter bleariness. I think he was trying to focus on his own smeared reflection: his drawn face and sweaty hair. Were they still serving, though? Stacks of empty glasses sat all along the bar, before the bowed and shadowed, sweat-greasy profiles of the other customers. The barman had his arms folded, his head tipped back.

At last my neighbour called out.

'Hey,' he said. And then, 'This – lady here.'

I tipped my glass to him when it came. 'Thank you,' I said.

By way of reply he nodded, took his first swig of his new bottle abruptly. He was sort of oscillating on his stool, gripping the bar with his free hand.

I drank half of my rather sweet-tasting vodka tonic, in measured sips, and didn't say anything else. My new buddy had started bobbing at the bar next to me by then, falling forward slowly, then rearing back slowly: a boat nudging its moorings at high tide.

'Hey, do you need to get some air?' I said.

He widened his eyes at that, and then lifted his hands in assent.

'Sure.'

He stood up clumsily and then I stood and finished my drink in one pull.

After we found his car we sat down together on the kerb there while he smoked a cigarette. By and by he lay back on the pavement, one hand behind his head, and with his shirt riding up, too, so I could see his stomach. He made a funny kind of effigy then, the smoke hanging over him in a moon-grey, graveyard fog. At last I had to pull him upright, and then his arm was slung heavily over my shoulder as I walked him back to my attic. He was dragging his feet. His shirt was gummy with sweat.

*

I came round at eight o'clock, to the sound of the pipes ringing out downstairs' showers. I was on the settee, and fully dressed. It was midday before my guest appeared from the bedroom. I looked up from my book to find him standing bewildered in the doorway.

'Hey,' he said, looking around the room, and then he blinked hard and then widened his poor eyes.

He was only in his underwear: blue boxer shorts and white socks hiked up on hairy calves.

'Hello,' I said, holding a hand up in front of my eyes, and then looking through my fingers. 'Why are you undressed?'

He tilted his head back.

'Um, I just woke up?' he said. 'Hey – you don't like this?' Here he rubbed his hand over his stomach, this action producing a rustling sound: he was very hairy.

I tutted.

'No,' I said.

'I'm just waiting till I go grey?' he said, 'because my dad is as hairy as me, but he's gone grey? He looks like a mouldy *nut.*'

Here he turned around and showed me his back – no less stunning.

Coins were spilling out of his pockets as he brought his clothes back out into the living room, they rolled along the floorboard cracks, then stopped there, like runners in a fairground horse race game.

'Goddamn it,' he said, bending to pick them up. Then he said, 'Hey. You want me to go, right?'

'Well – you'll have to eventually, I suppose. But not yet. Do you have somewhere to be?'

'No,' he said.

He pulled on his black jeans, buckled his belt. He put on his shirt and then lifted his right arm and gave his armpit a good sniff. Looking up, he raised his pale eyebrows at me again like he'd kept on doing last night.

I shook my head again.

'Um . . . Okay. I might need some coffee now,' he said.

'Go for it,' I said, pointing towards the kitchen, and soon I heard the cupboards opening and then the fridge door un-sticking.

'You have *no* food,' he said.

'No. I don't really do food.'

'That's a novel approach to life.'

'Mm . . .'

At last he brought two mugs of black coffee

in and sat down on the other end of the settee from me. He pulled his legs up and crossed them, and then he wiped his face again.

'Hey,' he said.

'Hi.'

'And how are you *not* hung-over?'

'I only had one drink, that's how.'

'Oh. Huh. Really?'

I nodded. He was looking at the grey soles of his socks now and frowning.

'Okay. Well, I missed that one. You don't like to drink?'

'I don't know if liking it comes into it, does it? I don't drink when I'm abroad, as a rule. I tend only to drink in situations where the worst possible idea would be for me to drink.'

'Oh. Okay. Well, I was shitfaced. I may have to puke soon. Hey, did I *drive* here?'

'No, we walked.'

'And *where* are we again?'

'This is the corner of Broad Ripple Avenue and Carrollton.'

'Okay. Not too far away.'

'No.'

'Did we talk at all last night, or . . . ?'

'We did. Me more than you, probably. Listen, can you remember my name even?'

He looked at me, didn't say anything. Then he winced, closed one eye.

'Very funny.'

'Your name is Aislinn,' he said, 'which is a Gaelic name meaning Dream Child.'

'Oh shit! I thought you were drunk!'

'And my name is ... '

'You're Drew. No meaning given. I was sober, remember.'

'Okay. Hey, was I being this funny last night?'

I turned my hands palm up.

'It's like that, is it? Hey, did I tell you why I was out? Did I tell you my story?'

'No, I don't think so.'

'About my mom's ex-boyfriend?'

'Nope. Tell me now.'

'Well, I'm going to. I couldn't stop thinking about this yesterday. Hence my um, condition. And this is a story about death. Is that okay?'

'Of course.'

'Because some people are squeamish about that.'

'Mm ... I've noticed that.'

I took a sip of coffee here, as he put his mug down on the floor.

'Okay. I'm going to have to relate some background first. This story put quite the spring in my step yesterday but then truthfully it began to weigh on me, so – then I got shitfaced. So – see what you think.'

'I will. Come on then, let's have it.'

'So – here we go. Um, my mom got back on – Friday, from visiting her sister up in St Paul, and while we were having dinner that night she told me that while she'd been there, Robbie Fitz had died. Or more accurately, he'd been found dead. So – who's Robbie Fitz? I'm terrible at this – storytelling. Okay, this is her first love. Her lost love. They dated all through college, and for a number of years afterwards. She married my dad, like – months after they split, so – take from *that* what you will.'

'Okay. Are they still together, your parents?'

'Ha! What do you think?'

Again, I turned my hands palm up.

'The answer is, *Hell no*.'

'Okay.'

'Ya, they split up when I was two? I grew up just with my mom. And she used to talk about this Robbie character a lot when I was growing up. Like – *a lot*. Anyways, they reconnected, or whatever, maybe ten years ago, although, not romantically, I should say. I think she met up with him when he was just divorced and he struck her as a little sad, or – not quite what she remembered. This is me reading between the lines.'

Here he stopped and set to scratching his frowzy right temple. The colour seemed to be beating in his cheeks again. He looked disoriented for a moment.

'Oh man,' he said. And then he said, 'Okay. I can't remember what she said at the time. But they didn't meet up again. Lost touch again, I guess, until – while she was up at Betsy's house, this time, there was this phone call, from *his* sister, asking how to get in touch with *my* mom, because he'd been found dead the week before. His neighbours had finally broken his door down, because of the smell, and the flies – I am *not* kidding, flies, and – he'd been lying there a long time. As in three months or more. You want to picture that?'

'No.'

'He was leaking into the carpet. You know that happens, right?'

'Yes, I've heard that.'

'Your body fat *leaks out of you*, okay? And your cranial fluids, your spinal fluids, stomach juices, your piss and shit? It all leaks out. You release a torrent of this stuff.'

'I can believe it.'

But Drew stopped short then. He looked over at me again and huffed.

'I'm telling this story badly,' he said. 'I am forgetting why it cheered me up.'

'Because he's dead and you're alive?'

'You think that's it?'

'Is that the end of the story?'

'No, it isn't,' he said.

'Is there a twist?' I said.

'Listen – let me just – I have to smoke a cigarette out of your window. Hey, where'd my cigarettes go?'

I turned around in my seat to watch him in the kitchen. He wiped the draining board with the stretched-out bottom of his shirt, and then hoisted himself up to perch there. I got up too, then, to put more coffee on. He was sitting back on his heels and smoking out of the window over the sink.

'This is ridiculous,' he said. 'I'm getting cramp in my ass.'

And then, 'Hey, whose dog is that?'

And, 'You must feel *isolated* up here, don't you?'

I shook my head.

'Not really.'

The dull little steel coffee pot was whistling

now, wobbling on the stove. It looked funny, like a toy.

'My mum had someone like that,' I said, 'a man called Anthony. It's a similar story, actually. She knew him at university, and they went out for five years. She got in touch with him again when I was thirteen, and later they met up. I waited up for them, obviously, creepy little creature that I was, but she came home alone. I asked her about it a few years later and she said, "Well, it was very sad, to be honest, very poignant, because although I found him *physically* repulsive, he *was* still my soul mate. He was still him." I remember thinking, No he wasn't. Another time when she told the story she was describing how she walked into the pub, that first time, and she said, "Oh, it was disgusting. This little old man jumped up and hugged me." That's charming, isn't it? Anyway, he died recently, too. He had cirrhosis, and there was no one at his funeral. Just his mum and my mum. But Mum's been married twice since him: to my dad, and now to this man Howard. She loves marrying these people. She said about Howard, "Well, it's someone to go on holiday with, isn't it?"'

Drew huffed. He dropped his cigarette in the empty sink, and ran some water on it.

'Okay,' he said, 'well, I'm done. Where were we?'

I lifted the coffee pot and turned off the flame.

'He was dead,' I said.

Back on the settee, Drew went on: 'Right. Let me get this straight. Um, so *his* sister was talking to *my* mom, and said that he'd really gone downhill after he'd been made redundant. Key word, right?'

(Here I found myself in receipt of another significant look.)

'Mm . . .' I said.

'He hadn't even tried to get another job. But, saying that, pushing sixty, I wonder what he could have got anyways. And he'd stopped eating, too. Spent day and night drinking and, um, phoning into radio shows? You have them in England? Of course, okay. Well, he would phone up these shows to talk about sports, Robbie in St Paul, on line one. I mean, it's pitiful. He had three kids, this guy. But turns out he hadn't kept in contact with them either.'

'Well, he would have been too ashamed, I expect, wouldn't he?'

Drew shrugged.

'How was your mum, though? Was she upset? Or was it all too long ago?'

'She said it was sad. I mean, I didn't want to

be prurient. Although – I guess I am, right? I've been thinking about it.'

'Mm . . . It does seem to have quickened your blood. Is that it, though? That's the story?'

'What's that?'

'Does anything else happen?'

'Okay,' Drew said. 'Did you not listen to what I just told you? This was my mom's lost love, going fucking nuts, starving to death, and then melting into the carpet like a burger on a grill. That story is *eerie*.'

'Is it?' I said. 'No, it's not. And you needn't say "lost love" either. I mean, come on. That's the original oxymoron, isn't it?'

He shook his head at me, and then yawned again, eyes closed, stretching his arms out in front of him.

I'd received one of Mum's texts about Anthony, the day after she'd got the news. She rarely texted and when she did, locked in upper case, everything looked like a telegram, or a headline, so:

ANTHONY ADAMS DEAD! FOUND LAST WEEK DEADFORWEEKS HOPE YOU ARE OKAY LOVEMUM x

I rang her as soon as I got that. I mean – she'd wanted me to, hadn't she? Still, she'd sounded surprised when she answered the phone, pre-occupied, as if she didn't know why I might be calling.

'Oh. Yes,' she said. 'Yes, that was sad news.'

I asked if she'd stayed in touch with him. I didn't think she had.

'Mm . . . I mean, I always sent him birthday cards and Christmas cards. Never got anything back though, so . . .'

'Are you okay?'

'Well, yes, I think so. I mean – it's strange. I don't know how I feel, really.'

'No.'

'I mean I had a *very* strange dream last night,' she said. 'We were together, Anthony and I, and just getting on *so* well, talking and laughing and *absolute* soul mates, and then I woke up, and I was just *so* happy, and then I thought, Oh, he's dead.'

'Right,' I said.

I could hear Howard's tuba in the background.

'Doesn't he ever shut up?' I said.

'Oh. Who? Howard? No, he doesn't. No. Never.'

8

There was a family crowd abroad in the park, strolling from craft stall counter to serving hatch in a new village of painted booths and prefab log cabins. Barbecue smoke laced the air and the wire bins were full of greasy-shiny napkins and Coke cans budding long wasps. Strapped in their buggies, toddlers in sunhats slept with their hands softly crabbed at their mouths, and meanwhile I had Cathy on the phone.

'Are you in New York?' she said.

'No.'

'Oh. Karl said you'd gone abroad.'

'Well, I'm not in New York. I'm in Indianapolis.'

'Oh. Are you with *Jim*?'

'No.'

'What are you doing there?'

'Not much. Walking home. I've been wandering around this art fair, or — art and meat maybe. I can see watercolours and rotisserie spits.'

'What's that?' she said.

'Oh, and here's a roasted pig,' I said. 'Hello there.'

This poor creature had been laid out with his trotters pettishly crossed under his snout, under the curds of his cooked eyes. His body was decimated, a basket of grey rags, but somehow there were still clouds of sweet steam pouring from his behind.

'*Pulled Pork*,' I said. 'Do you fancy a pulled pork sandwich, Cathy?'

'No.'

'No, me neither. Okay, let me just work out which way I'm going.'

'*Where* are you?' she said.

I looked down then at a portentous-looking scatter of little thigh bones in the grass.

'I've just told you,' I said, 'I'm walking home. What's going on anyway? Why did you call?'

'Fuck all.'

'Great. I'm so happy you rang.'

'Well – I don't know. Hey, don't be a bitch.'

'Won't this cost you a fortune?'

'No, it's fine. I bought a phone card.'

'I see. Okay. Hey, can you ring me back in about five minutes, then? I just want to buy a drink or something. I'm getting heatstroke. What time is it there?'

'Nearly ten, I think.'

'Okay. Cool. Ring me back in a minute then.'

There were no other customers inside The Bran Tub, only an ornery bustle of flies attending a counter still sticky with last night's sap. Leaning over the bar, I found a woman crouching bug-like in a corner, filling an unlit fridge with bottles of PBR.

'Hello there,' I said.

She winced as she stood, and then deepened her grimace as she cricked her neck. She was wearing a white, action-hero vest and her shoulders looked like unpolished doorknobs.

'Um, will you be wanting a *drink*, then, or . . . ?'

'I will. Yes, please. Can I have a fizzy water with some lime cordial in it please? Thank you.'

I took my glass with me out through their back door, back out into the sun, and sat down at one of the two picnic tables on their patio, in the shade of a dusty Miller Lite parasol. It was three o'clock and the sky was flame-blue.

Perhaps I should say here, that seeing Cathy's name on my phone's screen had been an unpleasant surprise. There'd been no formal break but we hadn't spoken in a long time. I don't think we spoke for a year before this phone call.

For various reasons. All that anxious business when I'd started therapy; how she'd followed me around then, that hadn't helped. And then there was what Karl had said about her, which had struck a chord with me, until all in all I started to see her as a real wobbling skittle of a liability in life. Was that fair? I think it was, at the time. And either way, there was a lot about her that had started to grate. Even down to her clothes: all those dressing-up-box outfits, the bell sleeves and high collars, they'd got less charming. And then those later adornments: that glinting St Christopher and then that heavy gold crucifix. (Where did she even get that? From a nun?) These were deeply tasteless affectations, I thought. I had no time for them, none at all – and none either for the concomitant wavering white smudge of a face she started presenting to the world then, down in the bars, with her voice looping ever higher, yes, just as the sparks fly upwards.

'I'm just waiting for Jesus to take me!' she used to say, in that voice like an out-of-tune piano, and worse, coyly: '*You*'d hate me if you knew where I went on Sundays!'

(I did know, of course, because she never stopped telling me.)

I don't know that I hated her, though. What I'd felt at that point was just, I'd say, a strong dislike, and also — consternation. A hot feeling and a cold feeling, a panicked feeling — that I could have wound up with this blown egg of a person going around claiming, 'Aislinn's my best friend!'

And later, 'Oh, Aislinn's *therapist* says she's not allowed to talk to *me* any more!'

'You sound like my mother,' I said.

So yes, I had disliked her. I'd disliked her to the point where this had happened: waiting for her in the bar one night, I saw — as was customary — her little black newsboy cap come bobbing into view over the mossy wall of the car park opposite. Biting on the rim of my tumbler, I narrowed my eyes at the blithe, religious jauntiness of this approaching hat, concentrating my malevolence, until — oops, it was gone! She really had tripped. I even heard her yelp. How embarrassing! Oh, how *nice*! I thought.

And this witness having imbued me with my own real sense of 'at one-ness' with the universe, I went back to my book with a smile on my face, only looking up again when she slid into the booth seat opposite me. We just raised eyebrows at each other then, before she leaned forward and started lifting up the mildewed grey storm-cloud of her petticoats.

I couldn't help myself. First I smiled — the smile was an unexpected twitch — and then I laughed through my nose. She looked up very sharply then; her eyes wide and shocked-looking. But then she had large eyes anyway. Large, *dog-brown* eyes. Yes, that was how I thought of them. That's what they kept reminding me of back then.

'*Don't* you laugh at me,' she said. 'I wouldn't laugh at *you*!'

(No you wouldn't, would you? I remember thinking. You're far too scrupulous.)

And then I held both my hands up.

'I'm sorry,' I said. 'That was involuntary. No, it was. It was the tension. I was going to pretend I hadn't seen.'

'Well,' she said, and she cast a wary, fugitive look around the room then pulled her heavily browed frown deeper, into a plunging flight profile, before going back to petting her grazed knees. (I had the impression, too, that she was holding back a really *big* burst of tears.)

But now my phone was buzzing and jittering again.

I answered.

'Listen, why in the damn hell are you my friend anyway?'

There was a beat. And then: 'Are you fucking kidding me?' Cathy said.

'Okay, how about this,' I said: 'if you've got nothing to say then I have. Guess who I saw a few weeks ago?'

'In Indianapolis?'

'Oh, where else?'

'Well, I can't guess.'

'I saw Morrissey. He was on just up the road.'

'Damn it. No way. I'm jealous now. How was he?'

'He was fantastic, obviously. What kind of a question's that? It was strange to see him, though. Here I am, alone on this continent, and then suddenly, there he was, too, proceeding through this – fulgent fog.'

'Did you get to the front?'

'I did. And he took my hand as well, so that was something. I almost called to tell you that, actually. He came and crouched at the edge of the stage, you know, as he does, and he was frowning down at me thoughtfully, singing, *And here I am* . . . And then suddenly he was gripping my hand.'

'Holy shit.'

'It was moving. I don't know. Sort of – even more moving than you think it would be. I always think I'm never going to see him again.'

'I always think that.'

'Mm . . . It's weird, isn't it? And that same hand held mine when I was seventeen, of course, so I was thinking about that, too.'

'Tell me that one again.'

'Well, that was in Chester. I got on stage, somehow, in the encore, and ended up on my back there being dragged off, but not before he leaned down and clasped the very tips of my fingers. I saw him upside down there, shaking his head at me, and singing, *Well never mind, never mind, oh . . .*'

'That's funny.'

'Mm . . . Was it though? But let me think. "Let Me Kiss You", that was good. He sang: "*My heart is open, to annie-one.*"'

'And the shirt came off.'

'The shirt came off, and floated gently over-head. Winging its way, damply through the darkness. Through the warm, quaking darkness of the Murat Center.'

'Ah . . .'

'Yes. There it goes . . . That was weeks ago, though. That was last month. But here's some other news: I have barely any money left, so that's on my mind, somewhat. Or it should be, shouldn't it? Or should it?'

'Oh . . . Shit. Well – I don't know. No one's got any money, have they?'

'Have they not?'

'Well, I haven't. My bank account's a septic sore. I've been living on bad cheques since February.'

'Really? Well, that's cheered me up.'

'It should cheer you up. I'm fucked. Yes, they all know my bright face in Albermarle and Bond. I go in, and they say, "Hi, Cathy! Are you treating yourself again?" And that's me: "*Yeah . . .*", and attempting this sort of rueful, naughty expression. Meanwhile I'm grinding my worry beads to dust. It's hilarious. No, it is! I feel like prey! Oh, but, saying that, I did have quite a sweet moment in there just after Christmas: I couldn't hold the pen with my frozen claw, so the nice lady came out of her booth and rubbed my cheque-writing hand between hers, rub rub rub, until it was all warmed up and – prehensile again. But everyone's at it. We're living in historical times, I think, aren't we?'

'Are we? Have you been buying batteries for your FM radio again?'

'Oh, you know. Not really. Maybe!'

'Well, either way, this is bullshit. I have to get a grip. I mean, I'm living in an attic in the rust belt, and it can't go on.'

'I know. It's— No, you're right.'

Here I had a long swig of my drink.

'I'll think of something,' I said.

And then, because she didn't respond to that, because there was only that familiar silence, that attentive silence, I went on: 'I'm supposed to fly back in a week, though.'

'Oh. Are you? That soon?'

'Mm . . . That soon. Which I will do. I'm not going to stay here and officially illegitimatise myself, although – it's always tempting. I'm not going back there, though, either.'

'Oh – no, you mustn't.'

'I just said I wouldn't.'

'Okay. That's good. I've been thinking about this actually. You have to get away from here. Get away and do your writing.'

'Oh, fuck off.'

'What?'

'Nothing. You're funny, that's all.'

'Am I?'

'Sometimes you are.'

'Thanks. So have you been writing while you've been away?'

'There you go again.'

'What?'

'Nothing. Listen, writing wasn't what I came away to do.'

'Oh, was it not?'

'Having said that, I have done quite a bit.'

'What did you go away for?'

'Oh, I don't know. Same old reason. It's hard to explain, isn't it? Do you know this quote: "I cannot afford the luxury of a self"?'

'No. Who's that?'

'That is Philip Roth. I like it a lot. I've been thinking about it, in my attic.'

'Okay.'

'Thinking that maybe through some process of triangulation I could elicit something that's me, but even that – thing – might only really be appreciable by way of Perseus's shield. And am I even that interested in it? Maybe. But quite possibly not. I think it might be lost now, but then I wonder if it was ever relevant. I mean, I'm not sure it's ourselves we're seeking, is it? I'd like to think it is, but . . . Well, I have all sorts of ideas.'

'Mm . . .' Cathy said.

And then she said, 'I feel the same, actually. I'm not me, either.'

'No?'

'No, listen, I'm *really* not.'

'Okay. Well – so much for that, then. How about this, though? I mean, this is a tiny example, but I've been thinking about this, too. It is germane. Do you know when men say your full name sometimes?'

'Yes.'

'What do you think of that?'

'Oh. Well, it depends.'

'Do you think so? Expand on that.'

'Well, obviously if it's some loser trying to make a point, then – that's hateful. "Well hello, Cathy Murphy." Fuck off. "Oh, look, if it isn't Miss Cathy Murphy." Get lost. Fuck yourself.'

'Yes, that is hateful. I used to get that a lot. Men trying to corral you, make your own name into a trick question or a snare. It's disgusting. There's something so – sweaty about it.'

'Yes, I hate it.'

'But then, this happened, too – it's quite grim to relate – I slept with this man in London before I came away, and that's the first thing he said in

179

the morning. "*Aislinn Kelly!*" It made me feel sick.'

'Was this Karl's friend?'

'It was. How d'you know that?'

'Well – Karl told me.'

'Oh, great. Anything else?'

'No. Don't be like that. He just said he'd introduced you to his actor friend. Larry, was it?'

'Yeah, Larry. They're all called Larry.'

'Oh. Okay.'

'No, his name was Lachlan. He was this big, posh fellow. Pretty fit, as it goes. I have very little memory of sleeping with him, though. Let's say it was like – Sophocles' off-stage violence. I don't know. My blackout metastasised. But, he seemed all right, until he lay back and shook his head . . .'

'*Aislinn Kelly!*'

'Mm . . . It was so sad-making. The whole thing was.'

'Oh. Was it? I've had that. I think it just means they're trying to – encapsulate you, doesn't it? If they say that in the morning. It's like they're saying, *Creature!*'

'It's the same thing, though, isn't it? That's the point. Encapsulate, corral . . . And it can't be got over, even for one night. After he'd said it, I rolled away to have a think and then he said, "Oh, she's away! Off again! But what's this? Hold still, honey, you've got a condom wrapper stuck to your back. My my. It's like a little, trampled flag."'

'Ah. That's nice.'

'You think so? Jesus. Anyway, that's just one example . . . Let's change the subject. Or can I let you go now? Are you yawning?'

'Am I?' she said. 'Sorry, I am listening. Let me just – get another drink.'

So again I heard the silky spinning of the bottle top, and then a garble of pouring.

'I might get back in bed actually. This flat is too disgusting.'

'Are you still at the same place?' I said.

'Mm . . . Of course I am. It's a tip as well. It looks like a crashed mobile library. It smells rank, too. Although I'm blaming that on this copy of *The Scarlet Tree* that I don't know why I own.'

'Oh, well, they're ubiquitous, aren't they? I had one of them. All of those Sitwells smell like dying root vegetables.'

'Mm . . .'

'It's the smell of those basements on Charing Cross Road.'

'Yes . . . I've been clambering around while we've been talking. It is getting silly.'

'A general mess of precision of feeling.'

'Mm . . .' she said. 'What's that? Just a sec. Wait there.'

But in fact I finished the call soon after that. I pressed the button. My phone was getting hot, anyway. It got horribly hot if I talked for too long, almost seeming to prickle in my hand.

9

The bedroom felt different on my last day: dusky, and chilly. I could hear the old tree rattling in the yard. I wore my blanket as a cape to go out to the kitchen, and leaning out to pull the window closed in there I saw the street's laundry being tugged about on its airers: sheets stretched out and pulsing, white shirts and sports shirts parrying with unsteady currents. The sky was a purplish-grey; the clouds like huge cauldrons.

Still – the cloudburst held off. That wind even withdrew, for a time. It was much later, late in the afternoon, that I came round to the wash of rain: drumming on the skylight and slopping from the eaves. That was a dreary noise. I shivered as I set the coffee on the stove. Now the whole room felt dank, and the front yard looked mired: one big ochre puddle.

Back in the bedroom the walls were running with shadows, a cool, pulsing scend dripping dryly over the bed, too.

III

1

On Bold Street the rain bounced in snitches, like old jacks. Our attempts to share an umbrella had been hobbling, and now Karl stepped out alone. All he really cared about keeping dry was his cigarette. Wincing over the prow of his coat collar, his hair quickly plastered to his forehead, he kept his hands cupped at his mouth.

In the gallery stairwell, I shivered and stamped. Karl wiped his face, and then shook his hands, and then tried to wipe his hands on the stone walls. I could hear the party somewhere above us: jazz music, and some disinhibited-sounding laughter.

One flight up, I showed our damp invitation card to a bow-tied young blonde woman stationed at a trestle table, and she crossed our names off her list before handing us two raffle tickets each.

'They're just for drinks,' I said, as we walked on, down a long, white-walled, spot-lit landing.

Howard was rounding the banisters up ahead, his face grim.

'Oh, hello,' I said, lifting my hand.

He looked at both of us very coldly for a second. And then, 'Ah! Hello!' he said. 'Aislinn! The wanderer returns! The eagle has landed! Yes!'

'Hello. This is my friend Karl. This is Howard.'

'Hello,' Karl said. 'Nice to meet you.'

'Hello! Yes! Aislinn's friend!'

Howard was wearing a blue corduroy suit, a red shirt and a darker red bow-tie. His beard had been trimmed, too: squared off.

'Where is this party?' I said. 'How much further?'

'Ah, yes. One more flight! Keep going! Excelsior!'

He called out after us, too, as we started up the stairs: 'Ever upwards! Excelsior! Find your mother!'

'Fucking hell,' Karl said. 'I always thought you were exaggerating about him.'

I shook my head.

'Oh, no.'

The coat rail was already listing. I laid mine and Karl's wet things on a chair instead, and then held up our raffle tickets.

'You just want soda water?'

'Yeah,' Karl said, looking around thoughtfully. 'Thanks. I'll be over there,' he said, nodding towards a clear bit of wall. The room was crowded and I couldn't see Mum.

Making my way to the bar, I thought I could spot her colleagues, though, sitting on two tables pushed together, women in shift dresses and sparkly cardigans leaning forward to chat between men who were balding, baby-faced, incipiently paunched. One of them would be the dreaded Colin I guessed; Mum's co-cubicleer for the last three years, whose detailed plot rundowns of every DVD he ever watched she'd always felt so powerless to stop.

An archipelago of tables led around to the buffet, as yet unwrapped. Tethered to the table legs and chair backs were bunches of helium balloons: round, puckered pillows in sugar pink and sea-foam blue, they said HAPPY BIRTHDAY! and HAPPY RETIREMENT! The band had set up in the far corner: two seated guitarists flanking a stocky violinist, who stood. In open-necked black shirts and black cummerbunds, and silky, black flared trousers, they looked to be enjoying the music they were making. Stencilled on their speakers in gold spray paint: *DJANGO NOUVEAU.*

All of these people, though . . . The set Mum always shyly referred to as 'Howard's friends' seemed to be well represented: the brood of shabby Vanyas wandering around the place were surely with him, and then – would his family be here too? I know he had a lot of brothers and sisters: ten, originally, I think, although – had some of them died? I hadn't been paying attention. My two stepsisters I did recognise, from the wedding. The thin one and the fat one. They were standing next to me at the bar, looking unimpressed with their wine. Well – I'd found them to be pretty sour specimens too, that one time we'd met. I didn't care to talk to them now, even to say hello, and they'd have no reason to speak to me either, I knew, except to make a vulgar point of it. I wish I could have trusted them not to do that, but – I didn't. I was careful not to catch their eye as I waited. I kept my face nicely set.

At last, drinks in hand, I went back and found Karl, still leaning on the wall, already rolling another cigarette. I waited for him to finish that and then passed him his water.

'Thanks. I think your mum's over there,' he said, nodding towards the door.

'Oh. Right-ho. Come on then.'

Mum was standing by the coats, a small striped gift bag held up in one hand, and a large card held up in the other. She was wearing a new dress, or anyway – I hadn't seen it before. In dull bronze satin, with a scoop neck and a dirndl skirt, it was girlish, for her, quite doll-like. It made her look shorter, and smaller. Her grey hair had been cut and styled, too, smoothed into a glossy bob with a heavy fringe.

'Oh, yes, thank you!' she was saying, as we stood waiting to say hello, and then, as someone else, a tall old man in a tidemarked linen suit, handed her another card, I watched as, still smiling, she tried, horribly, to keep looking at him – 'Yes, yes!' she said. 'Oh, thank you, yes,' talking over him now, her voice clambering higher – as at the same time she half crouched and reached back to put the gift bag down against the wall behind her. There was a row of coloured paper bags lined up there, and cards pushed halfway back into their envelopes.

When I said hello she looked round, and looked unsure. Her cheeks were pink and her teeth were bared. Someone behind us said, 'Have you got a drink there, Caroline?'

'Oh,' she said, looking at the floor and holding her hands up, 'Yes. Somewhere . . .'

'Mum?' I said.

She looked up again, her eyes widened, and she put one hand on her chest.

'Oh!' she said. 'Oh, Aislinn! It's you! I'm sorry, I didn't recognise you then! Oh God! Sorry, hello!'

I leaned over and kissed her on the cheek, and then on the other cheek, awkwardly.

'Here's Karl,' I said.

'Yes! Hello, Karl. Sorry!'

And soon she was holding my present up in one hand and the card up in the other. Karl took the opportunity to gesture that he was heading out to smoke.

'Now. Have you just got back?' Mum said.

'No, I've been back a fortnight.'

'And have you got a drink? Do you want my tickets, I won't use them . . .'

'Oh. Okay.'

I felt her nails as she pressed the raffle tickets into my hand.

'Thanks,' I said.

But someone else was approaching now, a bald man in a turquoise shirt, a glass of pale wine in his hand and his mouth open in ecstatic greeting.

'Freedom!' he said, before kissing Mum on both cheeks. 'Freedom, hey!'

She smiled pleasantly, lifting her hands up, holding them in small fists by her bare shoulders.

'Yes,' she said. 'Yes.'

As he turned to me she put her hands down again.

'Is this your daughter, Caroline? Hello!'

'Yes, hello there. I'm Aislinn.'

'Well, we've heard about you, haven't we? I'm Lenny, hello.'

Now he was kissing me on both cheeks. He smelled very strongly of cigarettes.

'What a great party, Caroline! Don't you know a lot of people? I was just saying, I couldn't fill a phone box, me.'

'Yes,' I said. 'I was thinking that. Who are all these people? Do you know them all?'

'*Well* – this is what you get for working in offices for twenty-five years, Aislinn, isn't it? So there's an incentive for you! So, yes, work colleagues, and then there's the Vic Soc, and Mensa, and the IVC, plus Howard's got a big family, hasn't he, so a lot of them are here. Anyone with black hair and a white beard, that's his clan. Like badgers, I always think.'

'Right.'

'And – that's just the women!' she said.

'I knew you were going to say that.'

'Well – I knew you knew I was going to! So! Yes, I think Wendy's here, with her husband. Is that Wendy? I'm blind without my glasses. And then, yes, any men with white beards. I know that doesn't narrow the field too much!'

'Are you looking forward to your retirement then, Caroline?' Lenny said.

'Well, yes,' Mum said. 'I mean, it's daunting though, isn't it? All that free time.'

'Hey, free time's great!' he said.

'*Is it?* I don't know. You've always had your days planned out for you, haven't you? Working since you were twenty-one, well, since you were *four* really, including school. I know Howard had a wobble. I'm worried I'll have an existential crisis!'

'Ah, no, but you do adjust, Caroline, you do. I mean, I'm okay because I do my affirmations every morning, and that just sets the day up for me. That's how I regulate myself.'

As we moved away, towards the bar to spend her tickets, Mum's smile was fixed.

'Yes, I was counting the seconds until he

mentioned his affirmations,' she said, through her teeth.

And then, '*Now*,' she said, 'I think they're going to unwrap the buffet soon, but you have to go and ask for your vegan platter. We could ask now, shall we? I mean, you can ask for it any time. I rang up this morning to check and then asked again when we got here and it's all plated up.'

'Oh, thank you. Yes, let's ask now, then.'

'Good.'

'Don't you want another drink?' I said.

'Oh, no. I've had two and I feel a bit queasy. I've been so nervous all day I couldn't eat, so . . . Best not.'

'Oh. Nervous why?'

'Well, I was just sick with fear that no one would come! Especially with this weather. I was just doubled up with nerves. But I think most people have, so, yes. More than we expected, actually, looking at the list.'

'Who's that gloomy man?' I said, nodding at one scowling fellow, sitting low in his chair, on a table near the dance floor.

'Oh, I don't know. No, I don't recognise him. Maybe he came with someone from the Vic Soc? I don't think he's one of Howard's friends, is he?'

'He looks like one of those old-time gurners.'

'Oh yes, he does, doesn't he!'

'I don't like him. I think he's a potential rogue element at your party.'

'Rogue elephant!' said Howard, passing.

Now everyone was eating; the band were taking a break and stood near us with their plates, conversing in low voices, their three half-pints of dark beer on the window sill between them.

Nodding over at Mum, who was talking to Liam now, over by the door, Karl said, 'So are those two still keen on their mini-breaks?'

'Oh. No — they're not, sadly. Howard has a tuba these days, instead. The mini-break holds no lure for him any more. In fact, he has *two* tubas, Mum was telling me. He acquired a "rescue tuba" from one of his artistic friends who was going to steamroller it and frame it. Howard intervened. So — that's what he does all day now.'

I put down my empty glass and picked up my fork again.

'Do you want another drink?' Karl said.

'Mm . . . Yes, please. This is stressful.'

'It is. I think you're doing well, though, for whatever that's worth.'

'Well, I'm relaxing into it, aren't I?'

'Yeah. That's always my advice . . . '

Later, in the queue to the Ladies I was accosted by this woman who looked to be dressed for a summer wedding. She smelled like the garden at a stately home.

'Ah, doesn't your mum look pretty?' she said.

'Yes,' I said.

'Ah, yes. She's been looking forward to retiring, hasn't she?'

'Has she? I don't know. Do you work with her?'

'Yes, we're all here from work,' she said. 'Well, all except Alison. Did she tell you about Alison?'

'No,' I said.

(All I really knew about Mum's work was Colin. Although, giving me a lift into town earlier in the year she had detoured to show us her office.

'Okay,' she'd said, 'coming up on the left here. This is where I toil away.' And I'd turned to look at a grey, pebble-dashed building banded with long windows fitted with vertical blinds.

'There!' Mum said. 'Fourth floor. There's our window! Look, Howard. Six more months to go.

Can't *wait*. Six more months of sorrow. Oh, look, Howard!'

He didn't look. It didn't occur to him to look, I realised. He was gazing straight ahead and working his jaw. I remember wondering: Did he have that tuba mouthpiece in his pocket? Or what?)

When I got out of the toilet, Mum's oldest friend Sal was waiting in the queue. Another person I hadn't seen since I'd left home.

'Well, I bought her a newspaper from the day she was *born*,' she told me. '*And*, just for a laugh, an inflatable Zimmer frame!'

Karl was leaning on the same bit of wall where I'd left him. I leaned next to him, and he rolled his head towards me and then narrowed his eyes.

'We can go soon,' I said. 'I'm reaching my limit.'

'Yeah,' Karl said. And then, 'Hey, have you seen this?'

He nodded at a small corkboard propped up on the buffet table, and pinned to it: a dozen pictures of Mum.

'Oh no, I hadn't. The many moods of Mum.'

We stood and looked at the pictures, and soon Mum joined us, on her way past with her empty plate.

'Ah, yes, poor little thing,' she said. And, 'Oh and that's on the beach at Morecambe. Sloppy Joe and pedal pushers. Every day, I wore that.'

'Did you pick these?' I said.

'Oh, no, Howard did this. His own initiative, yes.'

The photographs took her from toddler-ing to a year before she married Dad. Then: the lacuna; then: three photos from her and Howard's pre-tuba, mini-break days – the bistro years. Mum was alone in every one of these pictures, save the last, where she was with Howard. Again they were in a café, again both grinning horribly. They must have asked a waiter to take that one.

Karl said, 'Right. I'm going to go for a smoke if you're okay here.'

'I'm fine,' I said.

The band were back, two of them sitting down and strapping on their guitars while the fiddler took a seat at the piano. He struck up with 'Happy Birthday', played the opening bars a couple of times to ensure everyone had shushed, and then – everyone was singing along. And then it was: 'Hip hip!'

I looked around for Mum but couldn't see her anywhere, until – with the band playing together again now – I saw through the crowd, Howard pulling her around the dance floor. In a tango hold, arms extended, he steered her, and pivoted her, and tipped her, a painful death's-head grin on his florid face, and now their arms looked like a storm-wrangled ship's prow, and when I could see her face, she had her teeth bared, too, her eyes wide under that new fringe.

'Ah,' said Sal, standing next to me again now. 'Isn't Howard funny? Ah . . .'

'Yes. It's like Mum's a piece of furniture he's shifting,' I said.

I decided to go and find Karl. One flight down, walking back down the landing, there was a couple leaning on the table up ahead. I was halfway there before I realised it was Liam and his girlfriend. I could hardly turn around, could I?

'Hello, Liam,' I said.

At that he looked down and smiled painfully.

'Your man's downstairs,' he said.

'My man?'

'Your boyfriend, whatever's, just gone outside.'

'Oh. Karl's not my boyfriend.'

'Well, he's gone outside, so . . .'

'I know,' I said.

I leaned over the banister and saw Karl down there, shaking off the rain.

'Hey, Karl,' I called out. He looked up and raised an arm.

I turned back around. No one was saying anything, so after a moment I said, 'Are you going *grey*, Liam?'

'Oh. Yeah . . .'

He nodded forward, turning his mouth down at the corners as he ran his hand over his head.

'*Ah*. Distinguished,' his girlfriend said.

'It's stress, isn't it?' Liam said, still looking down, still looking grim.

And then, suddenly, Howard was there, among us.

'*A-ha!*' he was saying. 'Family reunion! You see – not that bad! Ye-es . . . The gang's all here!'

As his red wine slopped from his glass, with his free hand he was trying to operate his camera, now. Peering down into the viewfinder, he said, 'Hold that pose! Old grey! Yeah! Snow on the roof or what?'

Here he did his Woody Woodpecker laugh: a hiccup and then a bray.

'*Are ya ready for ya close-up?*' he said.

Karl stepped in then, in front of the camera.

'Oh, sorry about that, Howard,' he said.

2

Six weeks later: a blustery evening in Mossley Hill, and the streets still blotted from last night's storm. Unlatching the garden gate I could hear the same slow, parping tune I'd heard when I'd called Mum: 'Oh When The Saints', proceeding from the front-room window.

'Is it healthy him using all that puff?' I said as I hung up my coat. 'What if he has a heart attack?'

Mum widened her eyes.

'Ooh, fingers crossed!' she said.

'Now, what do you want to eat, Ash? I've got all sorts in, all vegan, and everything-free. Come and look. I got some of those gin and tonic cans, too. I'm never sure if you're drinking or not . . .'

Even with the TV on, and on loud, because Mum's hearing was going, we could still hear − feel − the tuba in the next room. We were sitting together on the settee. We both had cans of gin and tonic, poured out into glasses, on the go.

'Does he ever come out?' I said.

'Well – to eat, yes, and to use the bathroom.'

'Right,' I said.

'Like one of those – what are they called? They live up trees.'

'I don't know. Sloths?'

'Yes! Are they the ones? They just stay up a tree all week. Yes, the *three-toed sloth*. And I sit out here, fall asleep in front of the TV. Did I tell you he's got two now? Two tubas. Yes, I did, didn't I? I mean, why anyone would need *two* tubas.'

She shook her head again.

'But how's retirement going otherwise?' I said. 'Apart from that noise. Are you having fun yet?'

'*Fun?*' she said. 'Fun! What's *that*?'

'Well – are you?'

'We didn't have fun in my day!' she said.

And then she leaned forward and put down her little quarter-pint glass, and again, rubbed her hands together.

'Well . . . *No*, Ash,' she said, frowning now, 'I'm not really. No – I am – hating it so far, to be honest. Yes.'

'Are you? Oh no. How come?'

'Well . . .'

''Cause of him?'

'Well . . . I don't know. Not really. It is a big adjustment, isn't it? Having to find something to do with yourself every day.'

'Is it? There's loads to do. You had all sorts of plans, didn't you? And projects lined up.'

'I did, yes. I had a long list, but – I don't know. It is daunting. No, it is. I thought I'd go to the pictures a lot, but Howard won't go with me, will he? He just absolutely refuses, so I just go into town on my own, and sit there in FACT on my own, and then come back, and there's no one to talk to about what you've seen, and you do wonder, what's the point, really, don't you? And when I go to these "Senior Screenings" they do . . . you just look around when the lights go up and see all these old people, and I just think, I *can't* be that old. I mean, I don't look like them, do I?'

'Of course not,' I said.

Although, honestly – I didn't know if she looked old or not. I find it difficult to look at people like that. Besides which – she was my mum. I thought if anything she looked younger than she used to. Wearing no make-up (not that she ever wore much) and with her hair pulled back into a ponytail, albeit a rather stubby one, and in her jeans and a shirt today, with the sleeves rolled up, she looked good, I thought.

'I'm sure you'll adjust,' I said. 'But you know, you're sixty, not ninety, you needn't hide in here, just 'cause he wants to. Do you want to hear his opinions on films, anyway? You don't. What's he got to contribute? And why this phobia of doing things on your own?'

'Well, he just hates all films, doesn't he? So . . . that's all he'd say. Yes, I hope it is just a wobble. I mean, I know he did get *very* depressed when he finished work, and he *hated* his job – well, I *hated* mine.'

'Right. Well—'

'I mean, people say you should do courses, don't they? Howard's got friends who are just addicted to the OU, but – I am quite sick of being judged, really. My whole life's been dead-lines, and presentations, and doing what I'm told and being *judged*. Do I really want more of that, just when I've got free?'

She'd been looking straight ahead as she said all of this, frowning down at a spot on the coffee table, but now she turned to me.

'I mean, how do you deal with it, hey?' she said.

'With?'

'With not having that — structure every day. That security.'

'Oh. Well — what is it you're meaning by security? I don't know that there's any such thing. And I don't know that I've dealt with anything. Arguably. I mean, look at me. I've fucked everything up. But then — I'm not without purpose. And I am my own person. Oh, I'd divorce him if I were you and have a merry time on my own.'

She smiled when I said that, painfully, and hugged her stomach with her folded arms. I saw her flex her feet in her slippers.

'Well — *no*,' she said. 'I think you look very nice, actually, recently.'

'Oh,' I said. 'What? Do you? Christ, you never used to say that.'

'Well, you must have smartened up, mustn't you?' she said, and she did give me a merry look then, and raised her eyebrows.

'You used to look worried and say, "Do they wear things like that in Manchester?" As if it were some distant and forbidding kingdom. It made me sad.'

'Well – it is! The big city. I like Manchester, though. I'd like to move there. Maybe after Howard dies I can. I *hate* it here,' she said.

(There was that word again. And she said it so amiably, too.)

'Do you?' I said.

'Well, I never wanted to live in the suburbs, did I? Yuck. Never wanted to be in the North full stop. Just, you know – had to move back. I loved London,' she said.

'Well – can't you move back there then – after he dies? I can't imagine Manchester being much better than Liverpool. Manchester was rotten. I was miserable there.'

'Mm . . .' she said. 'Well, I don't know. Oh, was it?'

'Oh, don't sound so worried, Mum. What's happened to you? Why are you being so meek? Why don't you go to New York for a month? That'll cheer you up. You can sublet like I used to.'

'Mm – on my own, though? I don't know. I'm a scaredy-cat, Ash; I'm not like you.'

'You are not a scaredy-cat. I think that tuba's giving you Stockholm Syndrome. Hey, what does he say anyway? Have you told him you're anxious?'

'Mm . . . I tried. But you know how he is.'

'Not really.'

'Well, he just says, "Oh yes, *I* felt like that." But he's got his tuba now, hasn't he? So he's fine.'

'Right,' I said.

'And he's a depressive, too, isn't he? So . . . not much room for other people's worries there really. Everyone's self-absorbed, as he sees it. "*Amour-propre*," he says. But he's the one, really, I think.'

'Yes,' I said. 'Well. Quite. Christ, couples are revolting. What does he think you're getting out of this arrangement, I wonder?'

'Well, I don't know,' Mum said. And then she said, 'I mean, one thing is he just doesn't get my sense of humour, so if I say something funny, that doesn't work, to start a conversation. He *never* gets any jokes I make. He just screws up his face and says, "Er, *what*?" Or, "What does *that* mean?"'

'That doesn't sound good,' I said. 'Interesting move, though, marrying a man who doesn't get your jokes. What did you do that for?'

She shrugged. 'Mm . . . Don't know,' she said. I wasn't surprised to hear this, though. All Howard's bonhomie without eye contact had always struck me as pretty inauspicious. The funny voices, too. 'Oh, he only does that when he's nervous,' Mum once told me, 'around *you*.' But thinking about it now, I'd never once seen the pair of them have a conversation where one or both of them wasn't airily putting on a voice. Maybe I'd let myself believe things were different when they were alone. A vain, expedient sort of belief, that strikes me as now.

And now Mum went on, and was at least more animated and at ease than when she'd been talking about being retired. In her old, usual, blithe way, she said: 'And he's always picking me up for things I've said when we've been in company, which is rare enough anyway these days. Last time Wendy and her husband were here he was hissing at me in the kitchen. Just furious. And when they left he was saying, "*God*, you were rude. *So* embarrassing. What the *hell* gets into you?"'

'I've never seen you be rude,' I said. 'He's being rude. Who speaks to someone like that?'

'Well, I don't know,' Mum said, leaning forward again, conspiratorially. 'But here's all it was. Last year when we visited *them*, down in Bath, we arrived and Wendy had asked if we wanted coffee, and then, what kind? Filter, or cafetière? So I said, "Oh, instant's fine." And – shock horror.

Instant? Oh, we don't have *instant.*... So this time when they were coming here, I made a point of buying in this *real* coffee, because we've got that cafetière but we never use it, and so — they arrived, and it was Hello and Do you want a cup of coffee, Yes please, and I just made a point of, Oh look Wendy, especially for you, *real* coffee, *no* instant here, and then I sort of made a bit of a performance of sneaking the jar of Nescafé back into the cupboard and, you know, quite ceremoniously got this bag of *real* coffee out of the fridge and put it on the tray with all the other bits. It was just a joke. I thought I was being quite funny, wasn't I?'

'I don't know,' I said. And then: 'Yes. You were. He got *angry* about that? Actually angry?'

'Oh yes — his *face*, my God. Furious. And as soon as they'd left: "How *could* you? What are you playing at? What's *wrong* with you?"'

'How awful. I'm sorry, Mum.'

'And calling me an arsehole and a stupid cow. "Fuck off, you stupid cow," he says, if I ever dare offer an opinion on anything. And a dimwit, he called me the other day. *Me*, he's calling a dimwit! *Me.*'

She was shaking her head.

'Okay, Mum,' I said, 'I'm not sure what to say.

This is the atmosphere you're living with every day, is that right?'

'Well, yes,' she said, nodding.

'And then you have to get in bed with this person every night. Jesus. I mean I never liked him but this is malevolent. You have to leave this man. That's my first thought. I know that's easy to say, but – is this how you want to spend your retirement? Or even another five minutes? It's beneath you. You can afford to go and you should go. You know that, don't you?'

'Mm . . .' she said, and then she went on: 'And you know I had to just nag and nag him about my party, because he thought he was going to go in his jeans and his fleece! You know, he just *refuses* to wear a suit ever again, he says, now he's retired. And I had to keep asking, *just for this one night*, please. But he was like that when we used to go away, too, going down for dinner and everyone else is dressed nicely and he's in his sandals. If I mentioned it he just said, "Oh, who cares!" and, "Not everyone's looking at us, darling!" And then, "Well, would you rather I just stayed up in the room? Go on your own, I don't care." If anyone makes any kind of effort he just calls them "posers". "*Amour-propre!*" he says. I had to just beg him and beg him.'

'Christ. What a vain man. He's the one who would have looked ridiculous, isn't he? If he'd shown up in his *Nuts in May* get-up. And what do you mean you had to beg him? You most certainly did not.'

'Mm . . . Well . . .'

She was sitting forward on the settee now, and sort of smiling; she had her shoulders hunched up. I didn't know if she wanted me to say anything else or not. Was it possible that she was just 'showing off' maybe, in that way that sickly couples like to? No, I didn't think so. So I had to give it another go.

'Mum,' I said, 'did you hear what I said? If he's abusing you like this, why stay? That doesn't seem practical, as you used to say. Or do you think it is? Because I'm sitting here feeling sick and angry and claustrophobic on your behalf while I'm not sure what you're thinking. I'm afraid to react as strongly as I want to in case you start calling me insane again or high-handed. I mean – I presume you're telling me this stuff for a reason, and in good conscience that's all I can say. Except maybe, in the shorter term, would it help if I came up more often and we went out to the pictures, or out for lunch? I can't bear to think of you here on your own being ignored and scorned every day. It's outrageous. So would that help? Or is that no help?'

She didn't say anything to that though. She just looked – fidgety. She'd started looking fidgety and uneasy very soon after I'd started speaking. The tuba had stopped, too. One of us probably should have noticed that.

'What's this?' Howard was calling out from the hallway. 'Visitors!'

'What's that?' Mum said, leaning forward and pressing mute on the remote. 'What's he saying?'

'He said have we got visitors.'

'Oh. Yes!' she called out. 'Aislinn's here!'

'Aislinn! Oh, hello!'

'Hello,' I said.

There was the sound of him having a coughing fit, and then he came in with his face flushed.

'Aislinn!' he said. 'The eagle has landed! Yes! To what do we owe this unexpected *patronage*? I thought you abjured the family seat!'

'Oh, it was just spontaneous,' I said.

'Spontaneous! Yes!'

'Mm . . .'

'Now – you've both eaten?'

'Yes, hours ago! It's nine o'clock, Howard. There's some left on the stove . . .'

I saw him take the lid off the pan, and consider

what he saw, before pivoting slowly on his slipper heel and opening the fridge instead. He stared down into it for a moment before pulling out the butter, and a fold of ham, a large tomato, and then a jar of mustard. He wandered off to the bread bin next and then reached up for a plate from the top of the dresser.

'Well, Aislinn was in London last night,' Mum said. 'Went to see her friend's play. You remember Karl, don't you?'

There was a pause.

'What's that?'

Mum sort of smiled, widened her eyes at me. Then she called out, 'Her friend's play. Aislinn was in London last night.'

'Ah,' Howard said. 'Yes! London's glittering West End!'

'Well, it was near there,' I said.

Mum shook her head again, as Howard sat down in the armchair opposite us and then pulled over a small table and set to making his sandwich.

'Now – we saw a play set in a holiday camp once, didn't we?' she said.

'Did we?' I said. 'When?'

'Well, let me remember. We saw it at the Everyman, with Anthony. Now, who was it by?

Let me just remember. Oh, it's Joe Orton, isn't it?'

'I never met Anthony,' I said.

'What? Oh Aislinn, yes you did.'

'No, I didn't. When?'

'Aislinn, he stayed with us for a week!'

'Did he?'

'Of course he did! Unbelievable. It's supposed to be me who's getting forgetful!'

She looked over at Howard then, looking mock-incredulous, eyes wide, but he was busy dotting mustard on one slice of bread. He was pushing his lips out as he did it.

'Okay,' I said. 'Really? I mean, I believe you.'

I honestly couldn't remember, and I was actively trying to now.

'We went to the theatre, you say?'

'Yes. On his last night. And for a meal beforehand. Me, you and Liam. I can't believe you don't remember! Do you not remember that awful meal? That cold place?'

I shook my head.

'Sorry, I don't.'

'Well – you never will now!' Howard said.

It took me a moment to take that in.

'What was that?' I said.

He was chewing now, but I waited, kept my

eyes on him. At last he swallowed, stretched his lips out, licked his long teeth.

'I said, you won't be meeting him *now*,' he said. He was looking over my right shoulder as he spoke, at the bare wall there.

'*Anthony* has left the *building*,' he explained.

'Dead and *gone*!' he said.

I stayed in their box room that night. Mum had put a towel out on the bed, and a T-shirt for me to sleep in. On the shelf beneath the bedside table I found a book I hadn't seen in years. *Heidi's Years of Wandering and Learning*, one of Mum's old books I used to look at at Grandma's house. I'd been very struck by its illustrations back then – just because they'd all been coloured in so nicely. I looked at them again as I lay there; at the dashes of royal blue crayon here asserting 'sky', here banding a milk pail or a goat, while elsewhere a rose-pink crayon had been applied, in ragged stripes of hard scribble, to Heidi's pert face. An attempt had even been made to copy that goat, with Grandpa's surer hand providing the model, beneath which Mum had drawn her own goat, again, very nicely, I'd thought.

I mean, of course all of this had been touching to me: it had been my meat and drink back then, hadn't it? Being affected like that; stoking that unstable tenderness and then struggling to contain it.

'Ah, yes,' Mum had said, when I'd showed her.

'Raw talent, that!' she'd said.

Later she told me that having read this book, at age five or six, she'd instructed her parents not to use her given name any more, but to call her Heidi.

'Oh, I just wouldn't respond to them otherwise. I *insisted*,' she said.

And did they do it?

'Oh, *no* . . .'

And, she told me, after she'd watched *Anne of Green Gables* on TV, she stopped calling them Mummy and Daddy, and instead called them Marilla and Matthew.

'Oh, and they *hated* that.'

All this told in the course of our more convivial chats when I was growing up. Which were guileless enough, I always thought. I enjoyed them, anyway. There was a nice pride and care there, (wasn't there?) in her evocations of her '*so lonely*', industrious little self.

Aged six, for instance, standing at the front-room window in the house in Tyldesley, watching the other girls from her school passing on their way to the church hall for ballet lessons: 'Yes, they'd all go by with their mummies, all laughing and chatting, and they all had these identical little round, zip-up cases with their ballet clothes in, and I was *desperate* to go, just *desperate* to have one of those little – cases, but yes, your grandma just said, "Oh, *why* would you want to do that?" when I asked. "What on *earth* would you want to do that for?" So, yes, I just used to do it on my own in the front room.'

'Ballet?'

'Mm . . . Yes, I'd hold on to the back of a chair as a practice bar, and then sort of – run about in little circles, on my own.'

'Oh, Mum.'

'Well, it was sad, yes.'

The school was Church Drive, where I'd ended up going, too, for a couple of years. The smell of disinfectant took her back there.

'Yes, that very strong, thick, sort of pond-green bleach. That and the smell of dust: those dusty little boxes you used to have to put your things in. If I smell that then I'm just back there and I just feel sick, completely *sick* with fear.'

'Goodness, why?'

'Well – I hated school, didn't I?'

'Oh, okay.'

'Well, it was more than that,' she said. 'It was more that I was just – never quite confident that I knew what was going *on*. What was expected of me, or what I was supposed to be *doing*. So, yes, I did feel – very nervous, and frightened every day. Very sick, yes. Not confident. And I was all on my own, wasn't I?'

I asked her once, I think when I was a teenager, if there was a reason why Grandma and Grandpa hadn't had any more kids. Did she know?

'Oh. Yes,' she said, 'I do know. *Well* – it was because your grandma just *hated* her brother Cameron so much, didn't she? So she'd always vowed *never* to have more than one baby.'

'Really? Why did she hate him?'

'Well, there was that whole incident with him putting chewing gum in her hair, wasn't there?'

'Oh yes, I remember that.'

'And then I think, well, the main reason was that as soon as he was born she was more or less sidelined, wasn't she, because he was a boy. He was just lionised and idolised, and got everything he wanted bought new, even though he was three years younger, while she was ignored and then – shunted off and brought up by her auntie. Aunt Emily Gertrude.'

I hadn't heard about that before. The chewing gum story I knew.

'Oh, he was spiteful,' Grandma would say. 'Sniggering at me. *He* wasn't sorry. He could turn it on and off like *that*. He did it out of pure spite because he knew I was proud of my hair. *Pure spite*. He was an absolute *bugger*. I had to sit there on the stool in the kitchen while Auntie cut off all of my beautiful hair. And with him laughing in my face the minute their backs were turned. And it *never* grew back to what it was. It *never* did.'

'So I think she just decided she didn't ever want me to go through that,' Mum said. 'Which is – sad really, because I would have done *anything* to have brothers and sisters. That's why I had Liam, because I didn't want you to be on your own. Seems cruel, just to have one, I always think . . . And I don't know *what* she would have done if I'd have been a boy because she always said she *never, ever* wanted a boy.'

In the morning, sitting in the kitchen after breakfast, Mum was chewing the last bite of her toast and though it was barely light outside, Howard's

221

tuba was already drawling away in the front room. It was time for me to go, but instead I pointed to a new picture on the mantelpiece behind Mum, of Howard's baby grandson.

'Is he all right?' I said. 'Are they meant to look like that?'

Mum widened her eyes and put her hand on her chest as she swallowed.

'Does who look all right?' she said, turning around.

'That baby.'

'Oh. No – that isn't a great picture, is it? Yes, I thought there might be something wrong, but apparently he's fine. They keep wanting to come and visit, but I'm trying to put them off, to be honest. Because he'll just hide in there all day, won't he, while I have to pretend to coo over this thing.'

'You don't want grandchildren, do you?'

'Oh. No. I'm not bothered really.'

'Well, that's lucky.'

'I mean, I *think* Liam and Becky will have kids,' she said. 'He was asking me about the cost of weddings the other day. He stopped asking when I told him how much they are! So, yes, I think they probably will. But – I don't know . . . Although I wouldn't *ever* want to be without you and Liam, I do think it's a lot to go through, really, childbirth.'

'Right.'

'I wouldn't like the thought of a daughter of mine going through that, no . . .'

'You see, I always suspected it was far worse than they tell us. It's that bad?'

Her mouth turned down at the corners then. She seemed to flinch at the memory of it. She looked worried again.

'Oh, yes, it's dreadful,' she said. 'Horrible. Well, of course it's horrible, when you think of what's happening to you.' Again she seemed to flinch. She closed her eyes for a second. 'No, I don't want you having to go through that.'

'I won't,' I said.

'Well, good. No, I think it's men who want children, really, isn't it? And then grandchildren. To carry on their line. Even Howard's mentioned that, his "line", and he's not interested in anything. And I mean, I only got married because your grandpa wanted grandchildren.'

'Did you? You've never said that before. They both hated Dad, didn't they?'

'Oh yes, they did. *Hated* him. But this was years before that. I think I was thirteen or fourteen talking to your grandma, saying something like, Yuck, I don't *ever* want to get married and have kids. "It's like legalised slavery," I used to say, because, the way she used to run around after my dad, I mean – it was disgusting. It wasn't right. But she just went mad, absolutely mad: "Oh well, you must, you must, your dad wants grandchildren."'

'How horrible.'

'And then, of course, the minute I married your dad, it was, "Oh, *why* did you marry him? What on *earth* did you marry him for? Oh, *anyone* but him."'

'Christ, Mum.'

'But they were the same with Anthony, really, weren't they? "*Anyone* but *him*. *Promise* us. Just *promise* us."'

'God. What a strange pair. There's something so – humourless about that as well, isn't there? I wonder what it was they were so anxious to safeguard?'

'Well . . . I don't know,' Mum said.

'*Their kind of people*,' I said and then I twitched my eyebrows at her.

'Mm . . . Yes, maybe,' she said, and then she lifted her chin and shrugged, tossed an imaginary mane of hair: a blithe parody of careless vanity, except – I'm afraid I didn't find it very funny, after all.

We talked for a little longer. Not much longer. The clock was on the wall behind me and knowing what time I had to go, Mum's eyes kept miserably darting to it while she pretended to listen to me. All she kept saying was, 'Yes, yes.' She was smiling painfully, her left hand gripping her right hand.

Aislinn Kelly *Various*

Dear Erwin,

Firstly — I'm sorry for the delay in replying. This must be the longest we've been out of touch (telepathy notwithstanding). So — how are you doing? And where are you now, I wonder?

For myself, I'm quite well. I've been away again, abroad all summer, but I'm back now, working again. I'm writing this on a train, having stayed at my mum's last night. I don't know that I've talked to you about her before, but the visit was sad. She even walked me to the station this morning — sadder still. I exerted the whole force of my will in the effort not to cry when she linked arms with me.

Their griefs will try and inhabit us like that, won't they? (I've been thinking about this a lot recently.) How his (my father's, I mean) scavenging loss became my own, for a long time, and now this:

her bewilderment — I might say her 'indomitable'
bewilderment — might seem to be laying claim. I
felt it in that hand on my arm today. When she
really goes I'm afraid it's all I'll be left with. Perhaps
that's right, though. Perhaps it's my due. So I've
been sitting here going over these same old questions:
are we supposed to outpace these shadows, or not?
And how do we do it? Because all of my attempts
so far seem to me to have been: blind, ghastly, savage,
panicked . . . A funny fairy-tale history of crude
banishments and heroic fixations. (Perhaps you're
even one of them. Are you?) But then — is there any
other way to play this game, once you've been bought
in? What do you think, Erwin?

I broke off there, though, and didn't save that
draft. I closed my computer and looked out
again at the cold country we were pummelling
through: the frost-marbled earth and the dark
stubble fields, the moth-grey mists wreathing
Shakespearian copses, and holding what felt like
the last light of the year.

I saw through that winter in the welcome peace
and quiet of my new situation. Working again.
My books around me again. I didn't, as it turned
out, ever go back to have lunch or go to the

pictures with my mum. After Christmas she sent me some links to flats she wanted to look at in Edinburgh, and would I go with her? But she didn't take that trip, in the end. The last time we spoke she said she couldn't ever leave Howard. She just couldn't countenance 'destroying somebody's life', she said.

What else is there to tell? Perhaps only this, for now: how one afternoon in February I opened my laptop to find this on top of my inbox:

Jim Schmidt *Are you alive and what are you working on*

I wasn't surprised to see his name. Not really. But then I don't suppose it's uncommon, is it, for something so longed for to seem perfunctory in the event. Stale even. Still, I can't pretend I was unaffected either, as I sat down to read what he'd written to me.

Hey there – is this still Aislinn?
This is Jim, reaching out, seeing if this is still you and wondering what you have been doing to pass the time. Wondering if you are all right.
I suppose I will keep this short, as I am unsure

this is even reaching you!! If this HAS reached you,
I hope it finds you in good spirits!!
  xoxo Jim

The email had arrived at eleven o'clock, which
would have been, as I later worked it out, three
in the morning where he was then. He'd moved
again, of course.

Acknowledgements

The author would like to thank the Authors' Foundation for a grant that enabled the writing of this book.

www.vintage-books.co.uk